FAMOUS

CANTERWOOD CREST

FAMOUS

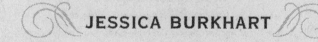 JESSICA BURKHART

ALADDIN M!X

New York London Toronto Sydney New Delhi

This book is a work of fiction. Any references to historical events, real people, or real places are used fictiously. Other names, characters, places, and events are products of the author's imagination, and any resemblance to actual events or places or persons, living or dead, is entirely coincidental.

m!x

ALADDIN M!X

Simon & Schuster Children's Publishing Division

1230 Avenue of the Americas, New York, NY 10020

First Aladdin M!X edition June 2013

Copyright © 2013 by Jessica Burkhart

All rights reserved, including the right of reproduction
in whole or in part in any form.

ALADDIN is a trademark of Simon & Schuster, Inc., and related logo
is a registered trademark of Simon & Schuster, Inc.

ALADDIN M!X and related logo are registered trademarks
of Simon & Schuster, Inc.

For information about special discounts for bulk purchases,
please contact Simon & Schuster Special Sales
at 1-866-506-1949 or business@simonandschuster.com.

The Simon & Schuster Speakers Bureau can bring authors to your live event.

For more information or to book an event contact
the Simon & Schuster Speakers Bureau at 1-866-248-3049
or visit our website at www.simonspeakers.com.

Designed by Jessica Handelman

The text of this book was set in Venetian 301 BT.

Manufactured in the United States of America 0513 OFF

2 4 6 8 10 9 7 5 3 1

Library of Congress Control Number 2013931643

ISBN 978-1-4424-3659-6

ISBN 978-1-4424-3660-2 (eBook)

Kate Angelella, of course this last book at Canterwood was always going to be for you. It exists because of you.
ILYSMYSB. xxoo

ACKNOWLEDGMENTS

Wow, I can't believe this is the last CC book (in sequence) before the holiday super special! Writing Sasha and transitioning to Lauren has been an amazing journey. Spending the holidays with them will be so much fun!

VIPs with an invite to Canterwood:

Fiona Simpson, Bethany Buck, Alyson Heller, Mara Anastas, Craig Adams, Valerie Shea, Jessica Handelman, Annie Berger, Katherine Devendorf, Stephanie Voros, Nicole Russo, Molly McGuire-Woods.

Stars in Canterwood's Hall of Fame:

Monica Stevenson, Alexis, Abril, Kyra, Aliyah, Dayton, Chelsey, Macey.

Author's Choice Award goes to:

The two best kittens—one-eyed Bella and Bliss. (Adopt a pet from your local Humane Society!) Every member of Team Canterwood from South Africa to California. Brianna Ahearn. Lauren Barnholdt. Alex Penfold. Ross Angelella. Joey Carson.

Golden Horseshoe Winner:

Kate Angelella. You've won the Golden Horseshoe for your stellar work on *Famous* from start to finish and your *parfait* line edits. As an editor, you grew this series from four books to twenty. Each piece of fan mail the author received should have been addressed to you—your hard work is spilled over every page of this novel.

And to all those who wrote thanking me for including Cole—you are so welcome. Please know that you are not alone if you are being bullied and TELL someone. Visit www.ItGetsBetter.org or www.StopBullying.gov for help.

I

TELL ME EVERYTHING

EVERYONE—MOM, DAD, BECCA, AND BRIELLE— grinned at me. They all stared, waiting for my reaction to Brielle's sudden proclamation. But I stood frozen in the Canterwood Crest parking lot. Brielle's words from seconds earlier rang through my head: *Now your bestie from home is here!*

Brielle didn't live in Union anymore.

She wasn't a student at Yates.

She didn't take riding lessons at Briar Creek.

As of today, Brielle Monaco was an official Canterwood Crest Academy student.

Blond Brielle, who'd just released me from a hug, put both hands on my upper arms and gently shook me.

"Laaaureeen? Hello?! Omigod, are you speechless or what?!" Brielle asked.

I nodded, furiously trying to form words. "I—oh my God—Bri—" I stopped and took a deep breath. Everything was finally starting to sink in. "Brielle Monaco, you go here now! This is the biggest surprise *ever!*"

Brielle laughed. "I can't believe I pulled it off. There's no way I would have without your parents and Becca."

"So many things make sense now," I said. "I couldn't figure out how you'd really gotten on campus for a family-only day. Or why you seemed so *off* at times. I can't believe two of my Union friends are here now."

Brielle frowned a little at my last sentence. I remembered her earlier fight with Taylor, my ex-boyfriend who was also from Union, and felt bad for bringing him up.

"We've got a *lot* to talk about," I said, slinging my arm over Bri's shoulder. I wiggled my fingers into my fleece jacket—the late November air was cold, and I wondered if we'd see snow at the Connecticut boarding school soon.

"We're going to leave you girls to catch up," Mom said from the passenger seat in our SUV.

"Have fun, you two!" Becca, my older sister, called from the backseat.

Dad waved, backed up the SUV, and guided the vehicle out of the parking lot and down Canterwood's driveway.

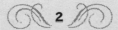

I hugged Bri, laughing. I tugged on her coat and pulled her in the direction of the dorms.

"Let's go inside before we freeze, and *you* are going to tell me everything," I said.

"Lead the way," Bri said.

Giggling, we made our way through the mass of students and parents who were headed for the parking lot and walked back to Hawthorne—my dorm hall.

"Take it all in," I said, breathing deeply. "Looking at this campus never gets any less exciting."

Bri's eyes were wide as she nodded. "I had a feeling that was true. Even though I was here all day, I don't really think I *saw* the campus for what it is."

We went up a winding sidewalk away from the stable. As we walked, we passed a pasture with turned-out horses. Two horses, blanketed, lay down next to each other.

"Aw, nap time," I said, smiling.

Bri asked me to point out buildings to her—even ones I'd told her about this morning when I'd given her the tour with my family.

"Of course," I said. "It would be insane to think you'd remember where everything is after an afternoon. It took me days of getting turned around to finally be able to stop sending SOS texts to Khloe that I was lost."

We passed the media center, administration, tennis courts, and finally reached Hawthorne Hall.

The three-story building was home to dozens of seventh-grade girls. Bri's eyes were wide as she stared up at the building. I could tell the realization was hitting her that *this* was her home now.

"As if this dorm isn't awesome enough, it also happens to be adjacent to Orchard Hall," I said. Goose bumps ran up and down my arms, but they weren't from the cold.

"What's the big deal about Orchard?" Bri asked.

"Sasha Silver lives there."

Bri's mouth formed an O.

Inside my dorm hall, I shook off shivers and stopped when we reached Christina's door.

"This is Christina's office," I explained. "She's our dorm monitor. Looks like she's gone right now, but I know you'll like Christina once you get to meet her."

"She sent me a few welcome e-mails," Brielle said. "It's so weird to be living without my parents. That part hasn't hit me yet."

"Oh, it will," I said as we made our way down Hawthorne's hall. "You'll miss them a lot, but being on your own is pretty cool. Except the stuff like laundry!"

Brielle and I walked into the common room, kicked off

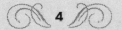

our shoes, and plunked down on the couch, facing each other.

"I almost texted all my friends, but I want some alone time with you first," I said. "Then we'll tell Khloe, and Clare, and everyone."

Brielle's brown eyes were wide. "Hopefully, they'll be as happy as you are that I'm staying."

"Of course they will be," I said. "They barely had five seconds with you, but I could tell they loved you."

Today had been the definition of insanity. Parents who had decided to go out on their own had wandered around with lost looks on their faces. Some had reminded me of what my mom and dad had taught me to do when I was little. The parents had sat on a bench, not moving, just waiting for their kid to find them. It was like I'd been taught—stay where you are and Mom and Dad will find you.

I'd barely seen any of my friends today, and we'd all had a lot less time together than we'd planned. It seemed like parents took over as priority, and everyone had a different way of handling their family.

I stood, unzipped my coat, and tossed it onto a nearby recliner. I was happy that the common room was empty. Brielle and I could openly talk in private.

"Before we start talking," I said, "want a cup of tea?"

"There's my LT!" Brielle said. "I'd love a cup of whatever you're having."

With a smile, I made us both one of my fall favorites—apple spice.

"Okay," I said. I pulled an orange throw blanket over my legs and raised my mug to my lips. "Start at the beginning and tell me everything."

2

HOW'D YOU
DO IT?

BRIELLE SIPPED THE TEA I'D MADE HER AND gave me an appreciative smile.

"I missed this," she said. "You making tea for us. I tried to make a cup after you left, and it was *so* gross! I mean, I don't know how you mess up tea, but I did!"

This I had to hear more about. "How'd you make it exactly?" I asked.

Brielle rolled her eyes to the ceiling. "Um, poured water into a mug. Dropped in my tea bag. Put it in the microwave for a minute and a half. Took it out and added a pack of Splenda."

"Oh, sweetie," I said, reaching over from my end of the couch to pat her leg. "No tea bags in the microwave, remember?"

Bri smacked her forehead with her hand. "Duh! Ugh! No wonder the tea tasted like burned rubber. Ick."

"Well, I'm here now, so I can service all of your tea-making needs," I said. "Now tell me, *how* did you get here?"

"It wasn't easy," Brielle said. "But I talked to my parents a lot about what I wanted for myself. What they wanted for me. You know my parents—they've always been concerned that I don't take school seriously enough. At first, they were convinced I only wanted to go to boarding school so that I could goof off more and get out from under their roof."

"That does sound like your parents," I said. "Have to admit, though; you don't have the, erm, *best* track record with grades."

Brielle raised her tea mug. "I take total responsibility for that and accept it. I wasn't a model student at Yates. I did the bare minimum to get by and used you and Ana a lot for help. I fessed up to my parents that I hadn't been doing my best." Bri took a sip of tea. "I told them I wanted a fresh start at a school that I already knew had a stellar reputation—Canterwood."

"Were they blindsided by the idea of boarding school? I am. It's something we *never* talked about. I mean, did

Ana know? Why Canterwood, really? Why even boarding school?" I had so many questions for Brielle. We might be in the common room all day.

"I want to let you know, first, that I didn't choose Canterwood to come and step on your toes. I know you've got a new life here. New friends, new riding circle—new everything."

I shook my head. "Please. I wasn't worried about that, and I don't care about stuff like that. You know it."

Brielle smiled. "I know. But it's just something I wanted to say. Boarding school has been in the back of my mind since you got accepted to Canterwood. I never brought it up to anyone because it seemed like such an out-there idea for me. My grades weren't that great at my current school, so why would I transfer to a *harder* school?"

I nodded, listening.

"Well, it's because of you, actually. You inspired me, Lauren. You were a model student at Yates and obviously a much better candidate for Canterwood than me, but you pushed me to want to try. I felt like I wouldn't get a fair shot at Yates because my teachers know me as 'Bri the kind of ditzy girl' and the boys know me as 'Bri the girl who is guy crazy.' Everyone has an opinion of me that I felt would be hard to change."

"I know all about that," I said. "Reputations aren't easy to change. I hate hearing you say that teachers think you're 'ditzy,' though. You're not, Brielle. I don't think any of our teachers ever thought that."

Brielle raised her eyes to mine. "If not that, then they definitely thought I wasn't working up to my potential. It was a repeat note I got on all of my report cards."

"I'll give you that as long as you acknowledge that you know you're capable of doing the work *and* getting great grades."

"That's why I'm here," Brielle said. "No one has any preconceived notions of me. The teachers will view me like a new student, and I'm going to work my butt off to impress them. I want a good reputation in the classroom. It just kind of . . . clicked for me over the summer that I was wasting a lot of time focusing on boys. They're just *so* not worth it right now!"

"Whoa!" I said, putting up a hand in a stop motion. "Who are you and what did you do with Brielle Monaco?"

Bri laughed. "I'm serious! Guys are great, okay, fine, but I was *sooo* obsessed with flirting and getting a guy that if I'd put half of that work into school and riding, I would have been getting awesome grades and would have been a stronger rider."

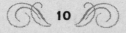

"Oh! I have to interrupt! It's killing me," I said. "Are you riding a stable horse? Which horse is it?"

Brielle's face morphed into a giant grin. "Nope. I'm not riding a stable horse. Laur, my parents bought Zane from Kim! He's coming today! I have my very own horse!"

"Omigod!" I squealed. "BRI!"

The albino gelding had been a school horse at Briar Creek for years. Brielle had been the one to ride him the most, and she loved him.

"I know! Mom and Dad said if I got bad grades at *any* point, though, the first thing to stop is my riding. There's no way I'm letting anyone take that from me, so you know I'm going to work hard."

"When did you apply?" I asked. I stretched my legs out on the couch so my left foot rested on top of Brielle's knee.

"I wrote a letter to the headmistress and asked if I could submit myself for consideration in August," Bri said. "It was so late in the year that I was sure she'd say no. I got an e-mail back, though, with the go-ahead to submit my transcripts and stuff."

"Did you tell anyone then?" I asked. "I wouldn't have been able to keep that to myself."

"I told Ana," Brielle said. "She told Taylor, but they were the only people who knew."

Students passed by the common room, laughing. Thankfully, the door didn't open and no one came inside. I wanted every second of one-on-one time with Bri that I could get.

"How did Taylor respond to your news?"

Brielle stared into her tea mug, then back at me. "He was totally fine with it from what Ana said. We still weren't speaking after the voice-mail fiasco. Ana said Taylor told her that he didn't care that we'd both applied."

"What about Ana? I feel bad for her! She's the only one of us left."

"I feel the same way. She was supersupportive of my applying and thought it would be really good for me. I could tell, though, that she was sad and hiding it. I'm just glad she has Jeremy. It's not the same as having a best friend, but they're close."

Almost two hours later, Brielle finished her story. I'd interjected every so often with questions. In front of us were two empty tea mugs—we'd drained two cups each—and napkins with crumbs from the kitchen's brownies.

This was a new side to Brielle. An academic-minded Bri who wanted to be a better student and rider.

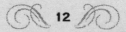

"After you see all of the cute boys on campus," I teased, "I give you three days before you're gaga for them."

We giggled.

"Nooo!" Brielle said, her tone a half whine. "Don't do that to me. I'm still . . . *weak*. You can't tell me about cuties this early in my detox."

I laughed so hard I felt my face turn red. "Okay, okay," I managed to get out between laughs. "No boy talk."

"Except about *your* boy," Bri said. She raised an eyebrow. "I never said I couldn't talk about my bestie's boyfriend."

The warm blush didn't fade from my face. I hadn't had much time during Family Day to talk to Brielle about Drew. Now I could talk to her all day about Drew! Maybe not *all* day, but . . .

"Look," I said. I woke up my BlackBerry, went to my "Drew" album, and set it on slide show. I held my phone between us, and Bri oohed and aahed at the pics. A lot were candids that I'd snapped of Drew swimming or riding. Some were of us that we'd gotten friends to snap of us together.

"Asking about Drew is dangerous," I added. "You'll have to slip me Sleepytime tea to make me be quiet after I tell you the fiftieth story about us."

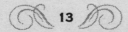

"Um, I'm still the same Brielle," she said, a wicked grin on her face. "I want to hear boy stories!"

"You asked for it." With that, I snuggled back into the couch pillow and told my best friend all about my boyfriend.

3

B + L = BFFS
4EVER

BRIELLE AND I STRETCHED ON THE COUCH, then stood. My phone had been buzzing with texts and BBMs—probably Khloe, Lex, or Clare—wondering where I was.

"I'm so glad we got to talk," I said. "I'm really, really happy you're here, Bri."

She nodded, sending her newly blond hair flying. "Me too! It still feels like a dream."

I took our cups to the sink, rinsed them, and stuck them in the dishwasher. "That's a feeling that won't go away for a *very* long time."

"I hope Clare likes me," Brielle said. "I did take away her extra room now that I'm her roommate."

"Oh, don't worry at all," I assured her. "Clare will love

you. She's a sweet girl, and she's probably glad to have a roomie again. You guys are a good match."

We left the common room and stopped in the hallway.

"I love you like crazy, LT," Bri said. She leaned forward, hugging me hard.

"Love you, too, B," I said, hugging her back. "We're going to have an awesome time together." We pulled back, still holding hands. "Do you want me to walk you to your room?"

Brielle shook her head. "Thanks, but I've got it. You go find your friends. I've got to unpack. Hopefully, Clare will be there, and we can get to know each other better."

With a wave, we split up. I checked my phone to read the BBMs.

Khloe:

Where r u? Everything OK?

Khloe:

L? I just heard from Clare that BRIELLE is her new roommate! Is that true?! Are u w Bri?

Lexa:

L!! Omigod, is it true abt Brielle?

Clare:

Whoa! I can't believe I've got your other BFF from home as my roomie! Did u know she was coming?! U didn't say anything so I'm guessing not. Like, SURPRISE, huh?

I locked my phone and opened the door to my room. Khloe, on her stomach reading *I Know Why the Caged Bird Sings*, righted herself onto her knees in a flash.

"Lauren! Omigod! Where were you?" Khloe's blond hair swirled around her shoulders.

I kicked off my shoes. "I'm sorry I didn't answer your BBMs. I was with Brielle in the common room." I flopped onto my back on my bed. "Talk about shocker. She enrolled at Canterwood. Two of my Union friends go here now."

Khloe hopped over to my bed, sitting beside me and peering at my face. "I think you're in, like, shock. Do you need me to use what I learned when I played a nurse in one of the school plays? I think I'm supposed to apply a cold washcloth to your forehead." She frowned. "Or is it a warm washcloth? Argh."

I laughed. "No washcloth necessary, Khlo. Thank you. I'm just taking it all in. That's what I was doing with Brielle. I needed to know everything about how she got here, from the moment she decided, to why she didn't tell me, and how she was feeling about being here now."

Khloe rubbed a clear tube of Urban Decay gloss over her lips. "I want to hear everything, but why didn't she tell you? Are all of your old friends from Union going to sneak-apply to Canterwood and surprise you?"

I grinned. "'Sneak-apply.' I like it. No, I think Ana's staying exactly where she is. As far as I know at this moment, anyway. You never know, obviously! Maybe my whole ex-class will end up here next year."

I sat up, folding my legs under my body. "There's so much to tell that I want to share with Lexa and Clare, too. But I'll retell the story to them. I was the most curious, too, about why Brielle didn't tell me. I mean, is there something about 'sneak-applying' that's popular? First Taylor. Then Bri."

"Exactly." Khloe bobbed her head.

"Brielle said she didn't tell me because she wanted it to be a giant surprise. She said there were days when she almost slipped and spilled it by accident and times when she almost picked up the phone and called. She said, though, that the idea of seeing my face when she told me that she wasn't going back to Union after Family Day was too good to blow."

"You were so caught off guard by her coming with Becca and your parents," Khloe said. "It was enough to keep your attention off even the tiniest suspicion that Brielle was staying. You were also running around like crazy showing things to your parents and sister, so you probably wouldn't have noticed if Brielle had dropped off a suitcase in Clare's room."

"Speaking of," I said. "Do you know how Clare is with the new roommate thing? I know she liked having the room to herself."

"I talked to her when we found out about Brielle," Khloe said. "Clare said she was just starting to get lonely in the room by herself. She's past it being Riley's space and was hoping she'd get a roomie, but she didn't expect it to happen until the new semester started. She's so excited that the person she got is a friend of yours."

I let out a breath. "Whew. I'm so glad. I think Clare and Brielle will be good for each other. Bri's a lot like you in the personality department, and I think she'll be a very . . . *entertaining* roomie for Clare."

We laughed.

"'Entertaining'? Hmmm?" Khloe gave me an *ooh this is news to me* face. "Is that how you describe me?"

"Along with superstar rider, Oscar-winner-in-training, and the best roommate a girl could hope for." I gave Khloe a giant smile.

She returned mine with one of her own.

"I'm going to totally quote you and put that in the signature of my e-mails," Khloe said.

I told her more about my talk with Bri. Khloe, always

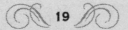

a good listener, nodded and *hmmm*ed along with every sentence.

"So, I've got to tell Lex and Clare. I want to do it without Bri being around. It would be too weird. You want to trail ride tomorrow?" I wiggled my eyebrows.

"Oh my God, yes," Khloe said, putting a hand across her forehead. "I'd go crazy if I didn't ride. I'm reading like a madwoman for English class, trying to get caught up on the parts of our book where I fell behind. It's a *great* book—it really is. But I need a break. I went from chaperoning my parents, which was so much work, to homework on the weekend."

KK pouted. "I haven't even been able to open my latest issue of *Celebs!* yet. That's how serious I've been about getting caught up in English."

"Whoa," I said. "You mean, you don't know if Jeni won *All Starz*? You can't tell me if Kris Kristopher is cheating on his girlfriend or if that was just a rumor?"

Khloe fake-sniffed. "I don't know *anything*. Not one thing about my world. My universe. I'm completely in the dark. I feel—"she took a dramatic pause—"Lauren, I feel like I don't know who I am right now."

"Oh, KK. Maybe you should reward yourself. After you finish reading a chapter for English, read five pages of *Celebs!* or something like that."

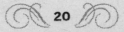

Khloe's woeful face broke into a grin. "This is why you're the genius in this dorm room! Eeeek! That's a fab idea, LT."

"Go get back to work," I said. "I've got homework too. I'm going to BBM everyone about the ride tomorrow, then start my work."

Khloe went back to her bed, rested on her stomach, and swung her feet back and forth behind her like a little kid.

I opened BBM and went to the group I'd created for Lexa, Clare, Cole, Khloe, and me.

Lauren:

Hey, guys! Sure u've all heard that it IS true—my Union friend Brielle is a CC student now & is Clare's roomie. I want 2 give u all the 411, so any1 up 4 a trail ride 2mrw @ noon?

My friends started typing seconds after I sent the message.

Lexa:

TOTALLY! I can't wait 2 hear everything! ☺

Cole:

Count me in! I want in on all the good gossip!

Clare:

Absolutely! Brielle's here, in my—our—room unpacking. She's SO nice, LT!

Lauren:

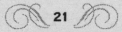

Clare—so glad u like her! I knew u would. U guys r going 2 get along rlly well.

C u all 2mrw! Meet KK and me outside of the main entrance.

I put my phone on my bedside table. I wished I could trail ride with Drew, too, but this wasn't really his kind of ride. He didn't need to hear me go on and on about my whole history with Brielle. Maybe we could hang out together later in the day.

I got up, walked over to my desk, and pulled my books from my leather Fossil bag. The Canterwood teachers were piling on the homework to prepare us for end-of-semester exams. The semester had gone by so fast—it was already mid-November, and soon we'd all be heading home for Thanksgiving break and then Christmas break.

Thanksgiving break sounded amazing, but thinking about Christmas made me a little sad. I was going to be separated from Whisper for weeks. We hadn't been apart since I'd gotten her. I wanted to share Christmas— peppermints, songs, lights, everything—with my horse. But I didn't think Mom and Dad would go for trailering Whisper to Union and boarding her at Briar Creek over break. Still . . . I wrote it down on my blue notepad to ask them just in case they said yes.

I had one more BBM to send, then it was work time.

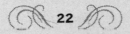

Lauren:

Ana-Banana, talk abt surprise!! If ANYONE else from Union is coming to CC u r under BFF law 2 tell me now. I almost fell over when B told me she was staying!!!! Now I've got Bri & Taylor even tho they're fighting. Bri told me about the voice-mail mistake—oof Hopefully, I'll get them 2 make up soon. Just wanted 2 say I hope u don't feel alone @ Yates. U've got Jeremy and u always have B and me even though we may not be right there. BBM me when u can, girly. Xoxo

I sent the message, plugged in my phone to charge, and mentally prepared myself for the mound of homework I had to get through today and tomorrow.

I put my math, science, English, French II, and history textbooks in a neat stack at the end of my desk. I flicked on my halogen lamp, and it cast a bright light over my desk. My cup of pen and pencils, notebooks, iPod dock, laptop, and framed photo of Ana, Brielle, and me on our horses at Briar Creek.

I got lost staring at the photo. When I finally pulled myself out of memories and looked at the clock, I hurriedly opened my history book and selected a blue Gelly Roll pen for taking notes. Things were definitely going to change around here. But I wasn't losing friends—I was gaining them, and the thought of Brielle being just down the hall made me smile.

4

PARFAIT WAKE-UP CALL

THE NEXT MORNING I ROLLED OVER IN BED when my phone vibrated. Blinking and trying to clear my hazy vision, I saw the notification for a new BBM.

Drew:

Morning! Hope this doesn't wake u. Wanted 2 say hi & say I heard abt ur friend from home enrolling. That's cool, L! I can't wait 2 meet her. I'll b @ the stable ltr, so mayb I'll run in2 u. Hopefully. ☺

I smiled at his message, pressing my face into my pillow. *That* was a nice thing to wake up to. I scrolled down, and there was a message from Ana. She'd sent it about an hour ago. Nine a.m.

Ana:

Laur, hey! Unless some1 I don't know has applied 2 CC, that's all of the Yates ppl u're getting! I swear! I'm staying here. With Jeremy. ☺ Not that I don't already miss B and still miss u. I hope B's transition is smooth . . . keep me posted. U & I will have 2 Skype sometime soon & catch up. Plus, I wanna c ur face! Miss u and love u! ~Ana

Ana's message made me smile too. I really had the best group of friends. I was beyond lucky, and I never wanted to take any of them for granted.

I rolled over onto my back, still snuggled under my covers. I opened Chatter and read through my friends' status updates.

BrielleisaBeauty: Unpacking in my new room @ CC & getting 2 know the awesome @CutieClare. I ♥ it here already!

TFrost: On my way 2 the pool 2 swim laps. I try out 4 the swim team 2mrw after class.

I read a few more updates from my old friends at Yates and people who were in my classes at Canterwood. I started typing my own Chatter update.

LaurBelle: Total surprise that 1 of my BFFs from home, @ BrielleisaBeauty, is a CC student now! So happy 2 have her here! Welcome, B! xxx

I started to put down my phone when it buzzed.

Becca:

On a scale from 1 to 10, how shocked r u abt Brielle?

Happy to see my sister's name, I immediately BBMed her back.

Lauren:

UM, 12!! U were SO good—u didn't give away anything. Neither did Mom or Dad. Sneaks. ☺

Becca:

LOL. It was 4 a good cause. Bri rlly wanted it 2 b a surprise. I got that. How's she adjusting?

That was like my big sis. Always checking on me and what was going on in my life to make sure I was okay.

Lauren:

So far, so good! Clare rlly likes her as a roommate. I haven't talked 2 B yet today, but I'll message her in a bit. All of my friends r looking 4ward 2 getting 2 know her.

Becca:

Yay! That's awesome! Brielle's the kind of girl who could fit in anywhere. Give her a week & ppl will totes 4get she was ever the New Girl.

Lauren:

U r so right. Hey, what r u doing 2day?

Becca:

Hmwk—blah. Then mtg Grant 2 go 2 the movies. ☺

Lauren:

*I'm doing hmwk too. Then trail riding with Lexa, Cole, Khlo, & Clare. Have fun w/Grant. *kissy noises**

Becca:

And NOW it's time to say good-bye! ;) TTYL. Love u!

Lauren:

LOL. Love u, Becs!

I got up and showered, and Khloe was back at her desk working. I needed to do homework too but realized I should BBM Brielle. I wanted to hear about her first night and let her know a group of us were going trail riding. I wanted her to know we weren't leaving her out—I wanted some time with my other friends to tell them more about Bri.

"YES!"

"Ahh!" I half yelled, jumping.

I whipped around to look at Khloe. Her brown eyes were wide, and she had an *oops* look on her face.

"I'm so sorry!" she said.

"You scared me," I said, putting a hand over my heart. "I assume it's good since you screamed 'Yes!'"

Khloe nodded so hard I worried that her neck would crack. "I can read five pages of *Celebs!* now!"

"Hey! Way to go!" I said. "Despite the near heart attack you almost gave me, I'm proud of you."

"Thanks, LT!" Khloe flashed me a smile before reaching down on the floor next to her bed and snatching up the latest issue of our favorite gossip magazine. She buried her nose so deep in the magazine that it almost touched the pages. Smiling to myself, I clicked on Bri's name.

Lauren:

Hey! How was ur 1st nite at here, CCA girl?

Brielle was probably still sleeping. She was a night owl and always hated getting up early for school. Maybe Clare's up-with-the-sun lifestyle would rub off on her.

I waited a few minutes, reading the news on my mobile browser, when my phone vibrated.

Brielle:

Totes amaze!!! Clare is the coolest. We had so much fun watching TV & she even helped me unpack.

Lauren:

YAY! I knew u 2 would get along. Clare's awesome. Were u surprised @ where u were when u woke up?

Brielle:

4 a second I was like—I'm still dreaming that I got accepted to CC. Then I realized it was real. LT, I was so excited that *I* got up @ 8!

Lauren:

OMG. Have u ever gotten up that early voluntarily?? LOL.

Brielle:

Never. I didn't WANT to stay in bed. I was 2 excited & there's a lot I have 2 do before starting classes 2mrw.

Lauren:

Speaking of stuff 2 do, I wanted 2 let u know that some of us, including Clare, r going on a trail ride this afternoon. I'd invite u, but since I got my alone time w u yest, I'd like some time w these guys 2 tell them more abt u and stuff. Is that OK? I didn't want u 2 feel left out!

Brielle:

Oh, no way—of course I don't mind! I totally get it. Only say AMAZING things abt me, tho, LT. ☺ I couldn't trail ride even if I wanted 2 2day. 2 much 2 do.

Lauren:

Yeah, I've got 2 get thru a pile of hmwk before tonite. It'll be so nice 2 have u 2 study w! I still can't believe ur here!

Brielle:

☺ I think I pulled off the most awesome surprise in r friendship history. *dances*

Lauren:

U did, hands down. BBM or call me if u need anything @ ALL, OK? There r no silly questions. I had sooo many. I want u 2 ask me if u don't talk 2 Clare.

Brielle:

serious face Promise I will. Thx, LaurBell. Have a good ride and say hi to Zane!

Lauren:

I will!! Xx

Now I was done with my phone. I wanted to e-mail Kim later this week and thank her for selling Zane to Bri. Everyone at Briar Creek knew how in love Bri was with the albino. It had been a while since I'd talked to Kim, anyway. I'd see her soon, though, during break.

I padded down the hallway, leaving Khloe to work, and went into the common room. I made a cup of green tea with lemongrass and ate a couple of scones.

I took the tea back to my room and set the cup at my desk. I settled into my chair and set my alarm clock for eleven thirty. I didn't want to get so caught up in studying that I missed trail riding.

I cracked open my fifty-pound history text and started scanning the section about the French Revolution. Uncapping my sparkly blue pen, I started taking notes. I was the Princess of Notes. Anytime anyone missed class, they always asked to borrow my notes. As I read, I couldn't stop thinking that Brielle was one floor above me. Smiling to myself, I wondered if Bri would be using my glittery notes later.

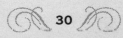

5

SIDE OF RIDING
WITH YOUR
GOSSIP?

WHEN MY ALARM WENT OFF, I'D BEEN STAR-
ing at it on and off for the past twenty minutes. I clicked
it off. Spinning around in my chair, I faced Khloe. She was
scribbling something in her leopard-print notebook.

"Hey, you want to get ready and head to the stable?"
I asked.

Khloe looked at the clock. "Oh, thank God! I was two
seconds away from dying, LT. You have no idea. Five pages
of *Celebs!* was a killer. It just made me want to read more.
I just got into the scandal about Reefer and Oliver and
then—bam. Page six."

I pouted. "Aww. That's *really, really* awful, Khlo. But
you got work done, right?"

A sheepish look came over Khloe's face. "I got a lot

of work done. I have one paragraph left to read."

"So the system works!"

Khloe closed her textbook. "It does. I was just being a brat." She winked at me. "Although maybe I'll increase my mag page allotment to six instead of five."

I shook my head, getting up and going to my closet for my riding clothes.

"Weather check?" I asked Khloe.

She grabbed her iPad and scanned it. "High thirties. Low humidity. My hair thanks Mother Nature."

"Thanks."

I pulled down a pair of tights to go under my breeches, a tank top, and a thermal shirt for layering and topped it off with a cable-knit Ralph Lauren Polo sweater. I reached into our mutual sock bin and found thick wool socks for my paddock boots.

Khloe and I were out the door in minutes.

"Brrrr!" I grumbled. "Cold sucks!" I adjusted my scarf.

"Totally. It's not even December and it's already this freezing. I bet we're going to have a white Christmas. The worst part, though?"

"What?" I asked as we made our way down the sidewalk to the stable. The sun blazed bright in the sky but provided no warmth.

"The worst part about winter, though there *is* an upside, is that you have to wear clothes, on top of clothes, on top of clothes, plus a coat, and you're so bundled up you almost have to squeeze through doorways."

That image made me laugh. "That's so true. What's the upside?"

"The accessories, of course!" Khloe shook her head at me as if she didn't know who I was. "Tartan scarves, knit scarves, beanie hats, trapper hats that are shaped like animals, Hello Kitty earmuffs, fuzzy boots. All things you can't wear anytime but now."

"Hmm." I tilted my head toward her. "You do have a point. I love the trapper hats that look like animals. I just ordered one from Shana Logic that looks like a unicorn! And I got a black beanie with sequins that's *très chic.*"

"Well done, *ma chérie!*"

The campus was more deserted than I'd ever seen it. Everyone was probably holed up in their rooms or in front of fires in the common room.

I heard hoofbeats before I saw the horse. Squinting, I saw a rider trotting a dapple-gray horse around the perimeter. Khloe's eyes were trained on the girl too. Long platinum-blond hair cascaded down her back. She was

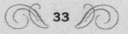

riding Rocco—one of Mr. Conner's stable horses. Rocco was usually ridden by *advanced* riders.

"She's not—," I started.

"There's no way—," Khloe cut me off.

"There *can't* be another transfer! Can there?"

Khloe shrugged, her eyes narrowing as the horse executed a *parfait* half-pass. Whoever this girl was, she was a *good* dressage rider.

"People can transfer in all year, but this year has been kind of an exception with late registration. We lost Riley, gained Taylor, and now Brielle's here. Unless this girl is here for, I don't know, a training consult?"

"We're going to wonder about this during the entire ride," I said. "Want to go up to the fence, say hi, and just flat-out ask who she is?"

Khloe made an approving face. "Wow. Bold move, Lauren Towers. Let's do it."

We walked across the grass to the large rectangular arena and watched as the girl put Rocco though a flawless twenty-meter circle. When the girl turned in our direction, she looked up, losing focus for a second. Rocco widened the circle, and she had to ease him back to the correct distance.

The girl patted Rocco's neck and turned him toward us.

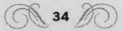

Khloe and I held up our hands in a friendly, we-come-in-peace-style wave.

"Um, hi," the girl said.

"Hey," Khloe said. She climbed up the fence boards and stuck her hand out to the girl. "I'm Khloe Kinsella, and this is my roommate, Lauren Towers."

I followed Khloe's lead and shook the girl's gloved hand.

"Nice to meet you. I'm Carina Johansson. It was really cool of you to introduce yourselves. You're the first students I've met."

She had an accent that I couldn't place. I'd never heard it before. It certainly wasn't southern, midwestern, or any of the other regions in the US.

"Oh? Are you a new transfer?" I asked.

Carina smiled. Her cornflower-blue eyes played up her pale skin. "Kind of. I'm a foreign exchange student. I'm from Sweden."

"Sweden?!" Khloe couldn't contain herself. "Wow!"

"That's so cool," I said. "How did you even find Canterwood?"

"My riding instructor knew about it. He keeps tabs on the best schools across the world. He knew I wanted to study abroad for a semester, so he suggested Canterwood

Crest. I convinced my parents to let me come near the end of this semester so I would have time to get used to everything instead of arriving in January when classes start up again."

I liked Carina instantly. From Khloe's posture, I could tell she was still unsure. I was willing to bet it had to do with the dressage.

"Those were some good dressage moves out there," Khloe said. "That's my specialty. Lauren's, too."

"Oh, how great!" Carina said, smiling. "Maybe we can all practice together for the advanced-team tryouts. Mr. Conner told me they're going to be held in January next year."

"Khloe's already on the advanced team, but I'd like to practice with you," I said. "I'm on the intermediate team."

"Awesome," Carina said. "Sounds great. Listen, I promised Mr. Conner I'd have this guy back soon in case he needed him for a lesson. I better go, but I hope I run into you guys soon!"

"Bye!" Khloe and I called.

Carina dismounted, adjusted her black North Face jacket, and began leading Rocco in large circles.

Khloe and I stepped away from the arena and toward the stable.

"Looks like we've got another newbie," I said.

A dark look passed over Khloe's face. "Yippee," she said flatly. "There are so many of them, if we get any more I won't be able to keep them straight."

"Hey." I elbowed Khloe lightly. "Don't worry about Carina. You saw five minutes of her riding. You don't know that she's some superstar dressage rider who's swooping in to steal the spotlight."

"You sure?" Khloe asked.

"No, *but* she is very likely a foreign exchange student who's here to learn about our culture and customs and ride while she's here. She must be a good rider to get in, but it doesn't mean she'll make the advanced team. Plus, she's an *exchange* student. She won't be here next year."

That made Khloe's face brighten. "You're right! Even if she's the school's best rider in history, she has to go home to Sweden at the end of the year."

I nodded. "Exactly. But we're still going to Google her."

We walked down the short gravel path and stepped onto the rubbed-matted concrete stable floor. I peered inside the stalls, and horses were in every color blanket— red, blue, black, plaid.

I followed Khloe to the tack room, and we lifted our saddles from the rack and placed them over our arms. Our brides hung from our shoulders. Fluffy, clean saddle pads were fished out of the bin and put on top of our saddles.

"See you in fifteen out front?" I asked.

"Perf."

We split up, and as I made my way toward the end of the aisle, I saw Lexa had just arrived too. She was bent over her strawberry roan mare Honor's tack trunk, looking for something.

"Hey," I said.

"Hey!" Lexa straightened, smiling. "I'm so excited about our ride, but *not* about the weather." Lexa had dressed like me—layers and a red bomber coat. She had black ear warmers over her ears.

"Agreed! If it's going to be this cold, it may as well snow and make everything pretty. Right?"

Lexa bobbed her head. "Totes. Instead we get brown grass, naked trees, and dead leaves. Ugly."

Whisper must have heard my voice. My mare stuck her head over the stall door, craning her neck toward me.

"Hi, baby!" I said. I disentangled myself from her tack and reached up to give her a hug and a kiss on the muzzle. Whisper was wrapped up tight in a hot-pink blanket. I scratched under her chin for a few minutes, and she started flapping her bottom lip like a fish. I giggled.

"Hey, Lex?" I walked to my roommate's stall. She was inside with the door open.

"Yeah?" Lexa was undoing Honor's purple blanket. The mare looked stunning in that color.

"You think we should drape blankets over their hind-quarters? Or do you think it's warm enough for them since they'll be moving?"

Lexa bit her bottom lip. "Good question. I actually could go either way. Want to ask Mr. Conner?"

"I'd feel better if we did. That way we're not worried about them getting cold."

Lexa let herself out of Honor's stall and latched it securely.

"We'll be right back, ladies," I told them.

Lexa and I walked to Mr. Conner's office. There was no telling if he'd even be there or not, but it was the best first place to look for him.

We passed the giant whiteboard in front of his office. I always read the messages. One caught my attention: *Sasha Silver & Callie Harper—see me Mon after class.* Eeep. I crossed my fingers for Sasha's sake that she wasn't in trouble. I'd heard Callie's name before. I was pretty sure she was one of Sasha's group. "Sasha & Co." was what everyone called them.

Mr. Conner's door was open, and he was at his desk. Lexa knocked on the door and he looked up, seeing us, then smiled.

"Come in," he said. "What can I do for you?"

Mr. Conner was as strict about keeping his office neat as he was with us keeping our belongings tidy. A giant Mac sat on his desk; he had a corkboard with a horse calendar pinned to it. There weren't any pens on his desk—they were all in a pen holder. Not a paper was out of place.

I saw the cast on his leg sticking out from the side of the desk. Just thinking about his accident made my stomach hurt. Mr. Conner had been teaching Sasha's advanced class last week and had taken them across the road to practice in a large field. Mr. Conner was also training Lexington, a young horse, for a client. Something had spooked Lexington and the horse had reared, flipped onto his back, and had narrowly missed crushing Mr. Conner's body. He did pin Mr. Conner's leg, breaking it. Mr. Conner was going to be in a cast for a while. But if you didn't see the cast, you'd forget there had ever been an accident. Mr. Conner moved around on his crutches almost as fast as he did without them.

"We're going on a trail ride," Lexa said. "I'm not sure, and neither is Lauren, if it's cold enough to put blankets

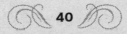

40

over the horses' hindquarters or if they'll be warm enough from the exercise."

Mr. Conner put down the pen he'd been holding. His black hair was cropped short, he had a slight tan, and he wore his usual hunter-green jacket with CCA stitched in gold lettering. The school's colors were everywhere!

"I'm glad you asked me," he said. "If it was a few degrees colder, I'd say blankets were a good idea. But you're not going to be out too long, I assume?"

Lexa and I shook our heads no.

"Then your horses are fine without them," Mr. Conner continued. "The movement will keep them warm."

We smiled at him.

"Thank you, Mr. Conner," I said.

Lexa echoed my thanks, and we left his office.

We turned onto the main aisle and almost smacked into Cole.

"Whoa!" Cole said. "Is there a sale at the mall that I don't know about?"

We giggled.

"Unfortunately, no," I said. "But go get your tack and hurry! We're meeting outside in fifteen."

Cole gave me a sharp salute, his face stoic but his green eyes smiling. Cole's infectious energy always made

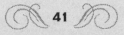

me smile. We could talk about anything—horses, cute guys Cole was crushing on—and we always had fun.

Back at Whisper's stall, I took off her blanket and folded it carefully. The blanket had kept her clean, but I whisked a body brush over her light coat. I picked her hooves and ran a wide-toothed comb through her mane and tail. In the stall beside us, I heard Lexa cooing to Honor as she did a similar grooming routine.

Whisper treated every grooming session like her own personal spa time. She let out grunts when I brushed her in a favorite spot and closed her eyes when I combed her mane. I loved making her feel good.

"All right, pretty," I said. "Let's get your tack on and go meet everyone."

Even though the stable had heaters, it was still cold inside. But once I'd started grooming Whisper, I'd forgotten about the cold. The exercise had warmed me up.

I placed a white wool saddle pad on Whisper's back, then gently put my English saddle on top of it. I tightened the girth to its usual notches and made a note to check it again after I bridled her. Whisper didn't move when I slipped off her pink halter. I took both of my hands and wrapped them around the stainless-steel bit, warming

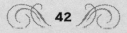

it before giving it to Whisper. With the crownpiece in one hand and the bit in the other, I slipped the bit into Whisper's mouth and eased the crownpiece over her ears. I ran my hands along the leather on both sides, making sure there weren't any tangled straps.

I'd taken off my solid leather reins and had replaced them with fun, rainbow reins with grips, which made them easier to hang on to when I wore gloves.

We walked out of her stall, and I stopped Wisp while I grabbed my Lexington helmet from my tack trunk. I put it on and snapped the chin strap. Gloves were next.

"And we're ready!" I said. "Lex? You all set?"

"Yep! Just need my helmet."

Lexa led Honor out of her stall, and Honor and Whisper sniffed each other's muzzles in a hello.

I loved that they were friends.

Together, we led the two horses down the aisle. Just outside the stable, Cole, Clare, and Khloe waited for us. Now we had *two* big things to talk about: Carina and Brielle. Let the gossiping begin!

HOW DO YOU SAY "STAR" IN SWEDISH?

CLAD IN MY PJ'S, I TOWELED OFF MY WET hair with a lavender bathroom towel. Khloe, already freshly showered, sat on her bed and watched the latest entertainment news. KK looked up as I came out of the bathroom, and smiled.

"Those pj's are giving me *major* envy," Khloe said. "Look at my eyes. Did they turn green?"

I giggled. "You know you can borrow my clothes anytime." My pj's were from Victoria's Secret's PINK line. I had purple leggings with an oversize long-sleeve gray tee with a giant glitter heart in the middle.

"Are we still going to do it?" I asked.

"Um, totes," Khloe said. "Whenever you're ready."

"I'm ready now! I want to see what we find out. If anything."

Khloe shut off the TV. "Oh, please. 'If' we find anything. Everyone has a past, and the Internet makes it oh-so-easy for us to snoop."

Khloe opened her laptop and patted the spot next to her. She was in pink leopard-print pants and a long-sleeve thermal shirt.

I settled next to her and pulled my damp hair into a sloppy bun—good enough until I blow-dried it.

Khloe clicked on Firefox. She went to Google and typed "Carina Johansson" into the search box.

We both leaned toward the screen. I scanned the endless links. The first twenty-something had nothing to do with our Carina, but with a famous actress. Khloe clicked the second page. Still nothing. More links to Actress Carina that shifted to Model Carina. None of Rider Carina.

"Ooh! Give it to me," I said.

Khloe slid the laptop in my direction.

"Let's make it a little more specific," I said as I typed.

I hit enter when I'd finished typing "Carina Johansson equestrian Sweden."

"Smart!" Khloe said.

We stared at the screen, watching the old page turn to white and a new page of links load.

Out of the corner of my eye, Khloe sat back a little. The same reaction I'd had.

"She's——," Khloe started.

"A Swedish Sasha Silver," I finished.

Neither of us moved for a moment. There were Swedish show results, some that I couldn't read, fan sites, newspaper coverage . . . everything a highly ranked rider would have. My stomach sank a little. The competition at Canterwood was already insane enough. Now we had *Carina*.

"Before we start looking at links and freaking out, what is Mr. Conner going to do with her?" I asked Khloe. "You've been here longer than me. What do you think?"

Khloe thought for a second. "Well, I think he'll follow the same protocol that he did with Brielle. He'll put Carina on the intermediate team and give her the chance to make the advanced team in January along with everyone else."

"She's an exchange student, though. Don't you think she'll go home in May?"

My mouth grew drier by the second. I couldn't think about having another strong rider like Carina to compete against for a coveted spot on the advanced team.

Brielle was already a strong contender, and she hadn't been here long.

"I don't know," Khloe said, shrugging. "We haven't asked her how long her exchange program is."

"I'll look for her and get to know her enough to ask."

Suddenly we both dove for the mouse at the same time, our hands clashing.

"Sorry," I said. "Your laptop. You go."

"We'll take turns," Khloe said.

Khloe clicked the first link. The website gave us the option for Swedish or English. Khloe clicked English.

"'Johansson Farms,'" Khloe read aloud. "'We excel in breeding top-quality Warmbloods. Our farm specializes in Swedish Warmbloods to suit your needs. Our horses have produced unmatchable breeding stock as well as sport horses of Olympic caliber.'"

"Whoa," I whispered. "Her parents are in the business."

I looked at the web page, and there was a photo of several huge stables, training arenas, and pastures. A sign, weathered to look vintage, read JOHANSSON FARMS in a delicate font.

Khloe scrolled down the page. "'We offer lessons to serious equestrians who are prepared to work beyond the traditional hours to further their riding career. If

interested, please fill out the online form, and someone from our stable will get back to you within two weeks. Please note that not everyone can be accepted as, on average, only fifteen to twenty percent of applicants are selected for admission.'"

"Click on the app just to see," I said. "I'm so curious."

Khloe clicked on the link for "Apply Now" and small sounds escaped both of our mouths. There were over fifteen pages of questions *solely* about riding.

The stable required a minimum of five years' experience to even apply.

"You take over," Khloe said, moving her hand off the mouse pad and drawing her knees to her chest. "This is the craziest thing I've ever seen."

I realized my hands were clenched together, and they were sweaty when I pulled them apart and put my middle finger on the track pad.

I went back a page and scrolled up to the top. I clicked on "Star Students."

Bingo.

"Look," I said. "Here's all we need to know."

There was a photo of a beaming Carina next to a gorgeous bay with a championship ribbon pinned to his bridle. CARINA JOHANSSON/WYNTER was typed under the picture.

There was an article next to Carina's photo, written in press-release style.

I cleared my throat. "'Johansson Farms is proud to be the home of Carina Johansson. At four, Carina began competing in local shows. Soon she progressed to regional, national, and eventually, international competitions. Currently, Carina is the title holder of the Juniors' All-Around Qualifier on her gelding, Wynter. See below for her full list of titles and past competitions. Carina is trained by Aksel Brunn, who is known for sending three past students to the Olympics. For press inquiries, please contact Carina's publicist at the information below.'"

I skipped over the publicist's information and scrolled to Carina's list of accolades. They blurred together.

First place, Grand Prix
First place, President's Cup
Sixth place, Swedish International Grand Prix
Second place at Gothenburg Horse Show (International Jumping)

The list went on and on.

Khloe let out a low whistle. "I am impressed. Not shocked after what I saw, but *jeez*. The girl is good."

Slowly I closed the laptop lid. All of Carina's titles ran through my head.

"Do you think she'll tell us on her own?" I asked.

Khloe leaned back against her pillow. "Maybe. But it's possible she's more like you than you realize."

"What do you mean?"

"What if Carina came here to get away from being that girl? What if she doesn't want anyone to know about her past and she wants to be judged on her riding at Canterwood?"

"I didn't even think about that," I said, stretching my legs out in front of me. "I was ready to go ask her about her background, but we just met her. If Carina wants us to know, she'll tell us."

"I think that's the best way to approach the sitch," KK said. "But it's good to know what kind of experience level you're dealing with too. You've been warned, so to speak, so you've got to be on top of your game."

"Absolutely. There's no excuse to be caught off guard."

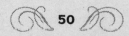

7

CRAZY CLARE

BY MONDAY, I WAS READY TO SHAKE CLARE until her curls came undone. Worst part? I couldn't talk to Khloe about it anymore. That's *all* I'd done over the weekend, and I didn't want to put Khloe in an awkward position between Clare and me for another day. All weekend, Clare had insisted that "something" was up with Brielle. I mean, I hadn't spent every second around Bri recently because things were C-R-A-Z-Y, but when I *had* been with her, I'd noticed nothing different. I'd known B longer than Clare, so if something was up, I'd know.

I plunked myself down on one of the cold stone benches in the courtyard. I pulled my down-filled scarf higher up around the back of my neck and blew out a breath. The Brielle thing bugged me. No matter how hard Clare had insisted there was something off with Bri, she hadn't been able to give me *any* concrete examples of weird behavior.

I pulled out my phone, scrolling to Clare on BBM and looking at the BBM convo I'd saved that had started the ongoing Brielle discussion. Clare and I had BBMed after we'd gone riding.

Clare:

I know this is awkward 2 bring up over BBM, but Brielle's here & this is ABT her.

Lauren:

What's going on?

Clare:

I hate 2 even say anything. I have 2 tho. Something's up w B. Did she say anything 2 u? Or did u notice anything weird?

Lauren:

No, she didn't say anything 2 me & I didn't get any vibes from her. Why do u think something is wrong?

Clare:

I'm not really sure. She hasn't actually DONE anything except for hanging up the phone rlly fast 2x when I came into the room, but I feel like she's hiding something.

Lauren:

I haven't felt that at all, C. Hmmm. I'll pay attn next time we hang out and c if I notice anything.

Clare:

Def do. I wish I knew what was up so I could tell u.

Lauren:

It's prob something so small—B can take stuff and blow it out of proportion sometimes. I'm not worried. ☺

Clare:

Okay. Just wanted 2 let u know.

That was only the beginning. Nothing had satisfied Clare. She gave up talking to me about Brielle and had started talking to Khloe. Then Khloe had talked to me. I'd tried to convince them both that they were wrong.

I'd watched Bri every time I got a chance today and hadn't seen one thing that made me pause. But my intuition wasn't enough to quiet my friends. I'd finally told Khloe that I was going to flat-out ask Bri if everything was okay. Then this discussion would be over once and for all. I planned to talk to Bri today after our lesson.

I quickly tacked up and headed for the outdoor arena. The jump course, just like in Mr. Conner's diagram, was waiting. I was the last of my teammates to arrive. I trotted Whisper into the arena and moved her next to Carina. Carina smiled at me from Rocco's back as we warmed up the horses. The gray gelding moved well under her. I'd started watching Carina more—there was a lot I could learn from her.

Carina was friendly, too. We'd ended up sharing a couple of classes and running into each other in the hall-ways. She'd always had a smile on her face.

Someone who hadn't smiled when I'd bumped into him in the hallway today was Taylor. I'd said "Hey," but he stomped off without a word. I didn't have the time or energy to find out what his problem was. Maybe he was mad at me by extension because Bri was here.

A cold wind blew across the arena, and I shivered despite my layers. I ran a gloved hand over Whisper's neck, glad that she didn't seem cold. Her winter coat had grown in, and the warm-up was keeping her comfortable in the November air.

Mr. Conner had e-mailed us a heads-up this morning. He'd sent us a note that had read:

> *Good morning, all,*
>
> *Please dress warmly for your lesson today.*
> *We'll be working in the large outdoor arena.*
> *Attached is a diagram of the jump course we'll*
> *be working on. Please look over the obstacles and*
> *familiarize yourself with the course before class.*
>
> *See you this afternoon.*
> *—Mr. Conner*

Khloe and I had spread our clothes across our beds, not wanting to freeze for forty-five minutes.

I wore a thin tank top, long-sleeve thermal tee, wool sweater, and my stable coat. Under my breeches I'd pulled on a pair of tights, and I had two pairs of thick socks on under my boots. It was a balancing act to dress in enough clothing to be warm, but not too much to be too bulky.

Wisp and I made a few more circuits around the large arena, moving from a trot to a canter, then back to a trot. A hunter-green beanie and matching coat headed for the arena. Silver crutches glinted in the sunlight.

Mr. Conner made his way to the center of the arena, a clipboard on a string around his neck. Lexa, Cole, Clare, Brielle, Drew, Carina, and I slowed our horses to a walk and lined up in front of our instructor.

Mr. Conner's black hair was hidden beneath his hat, and he wore gloves and a scarf. He removed the clipboard from around his neck and scanned it before looking up at us.

"Good afternoon," he said.

"Good afternoon, Mr. Conner," we replied.

Mr. Conner gave us a brief smile. "I hope you all heeded my warning and dressed for the weather."

Each of us nodded. I glanced down the line and saw

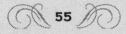

all of my teammates were bundled up. A head turned and Drew, sandwiched between Lex and Clare, shot me a smile. *Hi*, he mouthed.

Hey, I mouthed back.

Mr. Conner cleared his throat, and I whipped my head forward. My instructor's eyes were on me. I blushed and sank into my saddle. Mr. Conner stared at me for what felt like hours.

"Today," he said, finally looking away, "we'll be working on show jumping. Mike and Doug have assembled a ten-obstacle course that you'll each complete. I want to focus on your form and the amount of attention paid to you by your mount. In a moment, you'll all dismount and walk the course. If you studied the diagram that I e-mailed you, then none of these obstacles should be a surprise. After you've walked the course, you'll take turns completing the course."

The tiniest shiver ran up and down my arms. It wasn't from the cold. It was because of what we were about to do. I could jump a thousand fences, but I didn't think my fear of jumping would ever go away one hundred percent. The accident that had nearly ended my riding career was an invisible scar on my body.

"In addition to taking note of how you perform over

each obstacle, I'm also going to be timing your round," Mr. Conner said. "I want to add the pressure of getting a good time to make this exercise remind you what it's like to compete in show jumping. This will help you prepare for the show before break."

I inhaled deeply through my nose, letting the breath out slowly through my mouth. Racing the clock was what had gotten me in trouble when my accident had happened.

But you know better now, I told myself. *You've jumped a lot at Canterwood since Red Oak. You're not going to risk Whisper's safety just to beat a clock.*

"Please dismount," Mr. Conner said. "I don't want your horses to familiarize themselves with the course, so one at a time, hand your horse to a fellow teammate and go walk the course. Once you're finished, the rider holding your horse will go next."

I kicked my feet out of the stirrups, swung my right leg over the saddle and Whisper's rump, and hopped lightly to the ground. I eased the reins over her head and held them, waiting for further instruction.

"Cole," Mr. Conner said. "You're up first. Brielle, please hold Valentino."

Cole handed his black gelding to Bri, and the stark

difference between the horses caught my eye. Albino Zane looked even whiter next to black Valentino.

Cole walked to the start of the course, and his lips moved as he silently counted strides between jumps. The course was straightforward—there was only one turn—and thankfully, no switchbacks or change in order that needed to be memorized.

Once Cole finished, he took Valentino and Zane from Brielle. She walked the course as Cole had done, and Mr. Conner kept assigning pairs until each of us had been over the course.

We remounted our horses, and Cole was up first. The six of us who weren't riding exited the arena and lined up just outside the entrance. Mr. Conner moved to the fence so he wasn't in Cole's way. I watched as Mr. Conner produced a black stopwatch and silver whistle from his pocket and readied his clipboard.

Cole and Valentino waited at the arena's entrance for Mr. Conner's signal to begin.

"Cole," Mr. Conner called. "When I blow this whistle, you may start."

Cole nodded, his white helmet bobbing. He shifted in the saddle, and Valentino's ears pricked forward. Mr. Conner put the whistle to his lips and *tweet!* Cole and

Valentino shot through the entrance at a fast canter and headed for the first vertical.

"You okay?"

I looked over, and Drew had eased Polo next to Whisper. He kept his gaze on the course so Mr. Conner was less likely to catch us talking.

"I'm all right. Thanks for asking," I said quietly. "I was nervous before, but now I just want to go."

Cole and Valentino launched into the air and cleared a double oxer with gorgeous form from both horse and rider. They landed with ease on the other side and Cole did a half halt, slightly slowing an excited Valentino as they approached a triple combination. Cole was setting the bar *high*.

"You're going to do great." Drew sneaked a glance at me, smiling.

I smiled back, feeling my heartbeat slow a little from his words.

Meanwhile, Cole had maintained a clean and fast ride over half the course, and he and Valentino conquered each jump as if they'd ridden this course a million times. I was so impressed with my friend. I couldn't wait to tell him how awesome he looked out there!

Along the wall, Mr. Conner's eyes were glued to Cole

and Valentino. Mr. Conner held the stopwatch, ready to freeze the time as Cole approached the final jump.

Cole let out the reins a notch and allowed Valentino to quicken his canter as the pair neared the highest jump on the course—a tall vertical with black-and-white-striped poles. The jump looked simple and clean, but it was deceiving. If Cole let his guard down and Valentino rushed it, the horse would knock the pole to the ground. But if Cole didn't allow his mount to maintain enough speed, Valentino would likely bring down the top pole with a back hoof.

I held my breath as Cole moved into the two-point position and Valentino rocked back onto his haunches and pushed off the arena ground. Black mane and tail whipped through the air as horse and rider seemed as though they were trying to touch the cloudless sky.

"Wow," I whispered.

"Yeah," Drew whispered back.

Valentino landed safely away from the jump, and not one of the poles even so much as jiggled in their cups.

"Yeah, Cole!" I yelled, clapping.

Drew put two fingers in his mouth and let out an ear-splitting whistle.

The rest of my team cheered and clapped as a

pink-faced Cole slowed Valentino to a trot and exited the arena.

"Jeez!" Lexa said as Cole joined our group. "Trying to make it *impossible* for all of us to look good after that?" She grinned and high-fived him.

Cole laughed, then stuck out his tongue at Lex. "Valentino just wanted to *go*."

He loosened the reins and let Valentino walk in a circle nearby.

Mr. Conner finished writing on his clipboard and raised his hand to get our attention.

"Brielle," he called. "You're up."

Mr. Conner announced Cole's time, and I shook my head in amazement. Cole hadn't even been pushing Valentino too hard. That's what I liked most about the ride. I'd seen enough riders push their horses beyond the point of safety and past the horse's comfort level to get a fast time. I'd had to turn my head plenty of times when I'd witnessed a rider smacking a horse with a crop after almost every jump to increase the horse's speed. Each of us—myself included—carried a crop, but Mr. Conner would *never* allow us to get away with using one like that.

The whistle tweeted, and Brielle and Zane cantered forward. Brielle was a competitive girl, and as I watched, I

couldn't tell if she was ahead or behind Cole in time. Her ride was just as clean, and she and Zane were one fluid body as they tackled the course.

"Want to hang out at the media center after class?" Drew asked. "We could grab a private room and do homework, then maybe watch a movie."

I fought the urge to look at him and kept my eyes on Bri. "I really want to, but there's something I have to do after class. Can I text you when I'm done and we meet up then?"

"For sure," Drew said. "Actually, that'll give me time to meet my swim coach."

"Everything okay?" I whispered, cheering inside as Bri cleared the triple combo.

Polo stamped the ground with a front hoof. "My coach just wants to change my workout partner for the gym and give me a new spring schedule. Did Taylor talk to you about swimming recently?"

That made me look at Drew. "No. Why?"

"Coach Jenner decided the team needed two captains."

"You're still one of them, right?" I searched Drew's face. His eyes had darkened to a gray-blue. I remembered Taylor's Chatter update about swim team tryouts. I'd seen a recent note that he'd made it.

"I am, but Taylor Frost is the other cocaptain."

There was a hint of bitterness in Drew's voice. I couldn't blame him. He tried so hard in this beyond-bizarre situation of my ex-boyfriend coming to Canterwood and wanting to be friends with me. Unknown to Drew, Taylor wanted me back. Like, *back* back. As in girlfriend back.

Circumstances kept pushing Taylor and Drew together. They shared a few classes, and since they both swam, they were on the school's swim team. Now they shared the responsibility of being cocaptains together. Sympathy panged in my stomach for both of them.

"Drew, I'm sorry," I said. "You've been beyond amazing about the Taylor thing."

I closed my mouth when Mr. Conner looked in our group's direction. I put my focus back on Brielle as she and Zane headed for the second-to-last jump. Mr. Conner looked back to her, and I wet my lips.

"I feel bad that you guys keep getting stuck together," I said, my voice barely audible. "I'm glad you're still captain, but I'm sorry you have to share it with someone less than ideal."

"Thanks, Laur," Drew said, his voice super quiet too. "I have to keep reminding myself that it's more of a title thing and Taylor and I won't really be doing much together."

Brielle and Zane cantered, almost breaking into a gallop, to the final vertical.

Too fast, Bri! I wished I could tell her.

Zane reached the jump and took off a millisecond too late. He'd misjudged the speed and his closeness to the rails. Knees knocked on the plastic pole, and it tumbled to the ground as Zane cleared the lower rails and landed. I felt Bri's disappointment, but she eased Zane to a trot and patted his neck.

"Good ride, Bri!" I called. "You two looked great."

The rest of my teammates chimed in with praise for Brielle. She smiled and dipped her head at us.

"Thanks, guys," Brielle said when she was within speaking distance. "I tried to chase you, Cole, but I tried a little too hard." She leaned down, hugging Zane's neck. "You, mister, were perfect. You did everything I asked. That was my fault."

She started to cool him down, and Clare walked Fuego up to the starting point when Mr. Conner called her name. Pulling my bottom lip between my teeth, I waited for my turn while trying to keep nerves from settling into my stomach.

8

SO THIS
IS FLYING

FINALLY IT WAS MY TURN. I WAS THE LAST TO go. Clare had given a spotless ride but had the slowest time. Lexa had a clean ride and the third fastest time after Cole, who maintained his lead over everyone. Drew and Polo had knocked a rail in the triple combo but had a quick time. Carina and Rocco had been less than a second off Cole's time. I was proud of Cole for holding the lead over everyone.

I'm not going to focus solely on time, I told myself. *I want a clean ride* and *a good time. But no rushing.*

"Good luck, Lauren!" Drew said, giving me an encouraging smile.

"Kill it, Laur!" Lex cheered.

I halted Whisper just outside of the arena. She was the

youngest horse in the group and greener than the rest. I tightened my fingers on the reins and kept my legs loose against her sides. I didn't want Wisp to get a flying start, become excited, and then fight me to slow down and pay attention. I needed to start at a collected canter, and if she behaved, I'd feel out allowing her to quicken her pace.

Tweet! Mr. Conner didn't give me another second to overthink things. I urged Whisper forward, and she sprang into a neat, steady canter.

Parfait!

I sat to Whisper's even canter and lifted myself just out of the saddle into the two-point position as I gave Whisper a bit of extra rein. She pushed off the ground, tucked her forelegs, and jumped over the first vertical. Red-and-white poles were behind us and they stayed in their cups. But I couldn't focus on that.

Cold wind nipped my face as I prepared for the second vertical—a little higher and with white-and-blue poles. I allowed Whisper to increase her speed a tiny bit, and her stride lengthened as we reached the second obstacle. Whisper cleared the vertical like a horse that had competed a million times. Not like the five-year-old greenie she was.

We flew over the fake shrubbery, and I let out the reins

more as we made a long, sweeping turn to face the fourth jump. I gave Whisper even more rein and watched as she kept an ear pointed in my direction and one ear forward. *Whew,* I thought. *She's paying attention to me and the course.* I had control of her, and the oxer was in front of us before I knew it. I hoped the extra speed would help Whisper clear the spread of the double oxer.

She dug her back hooves into the arena dirt and pushed hard off the ground. As she cleared the span of the jump, I couldn't help it—I smiled. This had to be the closest feeling to flying. I kept my eyes between Whisper's gray ears, looking ahead. Whisper unfolded her forelegs and landed with room to spare on the other side of the oxer.

Seven strides until the trickiest obstacle—the triple combination. The jumps weren't high, but there was only room for one stride in between each jump before we had to be in the air again. Timing was *everything*.

I collected Whisper, softening my hands and slowing her stride. I needed every ounce of her attention on me. Whisper tossed her head and tugged the reins against my hands. She was excited and didn't want to slow down.

Four strides away.

Wisp, I tried to talk to her via ESP. *You have to listen. Slow down, girl.*

I did a half halt and pushed my body into the saddle seat. Whisper kept her pace up, then started to slow. An ear twisted in my direction, and I had control again. A trickle of sweat rolled down my temple from under my helmet.

Whisper couldn't have waited one more second to listen. We were at the first third of the jump. I didn't give her too much rein as she pushed off the ground and landed safely on the other side. One stride later, I moved my hands just slightly up her neck and lifted out of the saddle. Whisper's timing was perfect—she lifted into the air, clearing the rails, and came down cleanly on the other side.

A second later I asked Whisper to launch into the air again to complete the triple combo. She followed my instructions and snapped her knees under her, pushing off the dirt and leaping into the air. Whisper landed and I held my breath, but all I heard were hoofbeats as we cantered away from the triple. No rails had fallen!

I was *très* proud of Wisp. She had gotten out of hand and pulled herself together, listened to me, and had completed a complicated triple as if she did them every day.

I kept her collected as we took the next vertical, faux stonewall, and another vertical. Whisper didn't ask

for more rein or lose interest between jumps. After the vertical, I gave Wisp a little rein and allowed her canter to quicken as we approached the second-to-last jump—a double oxer. This one had a wider spread than the first.

Whisper breathed rhythmically as she moved, and I kept my eye on the oxer. I let out the reins a bit more, and Whisper swished her tail with excitement as she moved into a faster canter. We were at the oxer, and I lifted out of the saddle as Whisper surged off the ground and soared over the space between the rails. She landed without coming close to the rail behind us and tore off toward the final vertical.

I trusted Whisper. She was at a near gallop, but it was controlled. Wisp hadn't stopped listening to me, and as long as she didn't forget about me, I wanted to give her a little freedom. Wind *whooshed* in my ears as we swept past Mr. Conner. The saddle seemed to disappear between us, and it felt as though we were one. I'd never felt closer to my horse before.

The vertical loomed tall in front of us as we approached it. A tiny flicker of fear was extinguished when Whisper gave a determined snort, and I knew she was going for it. She wanted to clear the jump.

Just as we'd started, with little time for me to

overthink things, there was no time to overanalyze the final jump.

It was here.

I lifted out of the saddle, taking weight off Whisper's back, and kneaded my hands along her neck. Whisper thrust into the air using her hindquarters, and it seemed as though she was never going to stop ascending into the air.

A grin split my face before we'd even landed. When we did, I turned quickly and saw the pole was in the cup!

We'd completed a clean round!

"Good, good, good girl!" I said, patting Whisper's neck. "You were amazing, baby!" I gently pulled on the reins, slowing her down. Whisper's stride had an extra bounce to it—she *knew* she'd jumped clean.

Cheers broke out from the side of the arena. The clapping and noise only made Whisper's prancing more pronounced.

"Yeah, Lauren!" Drew called. He'd dropped Polo's reins around the gelding's neck and clapped.

"Awesome, Laur!" Bri said. She gave me a thumbs-up.

I pulled Whisper to a trot, then a walk, as we exited the arena and passed my friends. Whisper kept swishing her tail and lifted her hooves high into the air. It was as

if she knew her friends had been watching. I rode her up to the group and everyone surrounded us, offering me a palm to slap.

A shiver ran through me. This time from pure bliss—not cold or fear.

"LT, that was amaze!" Cole said. He held up his gloved hand. "I wish we had that on video."

A perma-grin was stuck on my face. "Thanks, guys," I said. "It was all Whisper. She's turning out to be a real jumper."

The group broke up to let me cool down Whisper.

"Lauren," Mr. Conner called. "Bring Whisper into the arena and walk her along the wall to cool her down. The rest of you need to line up in front of me."

I nodded and turned Wisp back toward the arena. I walked her on a loose rein.

Mr. Conner smiled at me, looking up from his clipboard. "That was a fantastic ride, Lauren. Well done."

I smiled. Praise like that was rare from Mr. Conner.

"However," Mr. Conner said, "I'm afraid your time was a half second behind Cole's. I hope you're still just as proud of your ride, though."

"I am," I said. "Whisper was amazing."

"Congratulations, Cole," Mr. Conner said, nodding at

him. "Your ride was not only clean, but it was also the fastest time. I'm quite proud of your effort today and hope you are as well."

Whisper and I rejoined the group, and everyone smiled at Cole.

I mock-frowned at Cole. "We'll get you next time," I said icily.

"I'd like to see you try," he said, playing right back.

Everyone laughed. Even Mr. Conner.

9

EVERYTHING'S
COOL . . . RIGHT?

AFTER I TOOK CARE OF WHISPER, I HEADED
for Zane's stall. Brielle, sliding the bolt to lock his stall
door, turned to me with a smile.

"If it isn't Miss I Rock at Show Jumping," Bri said.
She undid her long ponytail and let her blond hair fall
around her shoulders.

I shook my head at her. "Thank you, but we need a
zillion more rides like that to really qualify as 'rocking.'"

Zane poked his head over the stall door, and I reached
out to stroke his cheek. Brielle had a royal-blue halter on
him that looked stunning against his coat.

"What are you up to now?" Brielle asked.

"Hoping to chat with you, actually," I said. "Do you
have time to talk for a few minutes? I was thinking we

change and meet in the common room, maybe?"

Lines creased Brielle's forehead as she frowned. "Is everything okay? You're making me nervous!"

I waved my hand dismissively. "Oh, yeah. Everything's *totally* fine. I'll explain, but I just want to talk so I can basically make someone else stop talking."

We both laughed as I rolled my eyes at the awkwardness of my explanation.

"Sure," Brielle said. "I'll talk to you to quiet someone else. Makes total sense."

"Let's get out of here." I gently pushed my friend's shoulder in the direction of the exit. I looped my arm through hers, and Brielle and I chitchatted as we made our way across the frigid campus and back to Hawthorne.

"See you in five," I said when we reached the stairs.

"Four!" Brielle said, running up the stairs to the room that she shared with Clare.

I opened the door to my room, and it was empty. Khloe was probably still cooling Ever after their lesson. I purposely hadn't told her that I'd been planning on talking to Bri. The whole thing was so silly. After Brielle told me everything was fine with her, *then* I could report back to my friends that I'd been right all along.

I stood in front of the full-length mirror and checked my reflection. I'd slipped out of riding clothes and had slid on black leggings and an oversize lavender-and-white striped off-the-shoulder sweatshirt with ragged edges.

I grabbed a brush, ran it through my hair, and slid my feet into black ballet flats.

Brielle was going to beat me!

I hurried out of my room and almost collided with two other girls coming out of the common room. I peered inside and Brielle, sitting on the couch, gave me a Cheshire cat smile.

"Four," she said.

"You're fast and you look fantastic," I said, taking in Bri's outfit.

Like me, she was in leggings, hers gray paired with a bubble-gum-pink V-neck long-sleeve shirt. A long necklace—big aqua strands mixed with silver—hung around her neck.

"I got my speed from waking up five minutes before I had to leave for school," Bri said. "My fashion sense came from you, dear LT."

I put my hand across my heart. "Aw. You are my bestie."

I walked around to the kitchen and filled the teakettle

with water. This chat with Bri was going to be so short, we probably wouldn't even finish our tea here.

"Can I make you a cup?" I asked her.

"Please," Brielle said. "Whatever you're having."

In minutes I had two steaming mugs of white tea with blueberry.

"Thank you," Bri said as I handed her a mug. "It looks like you picked this one out just for me!"

I smiled. "That's because I did!"

I'd chosen a white mug with an aqua heart in the center. My mug was coffee brown with pink dots and a matching top with a space for a straw.

My tea was too hot to sip, so I set it on a yellow Kate Spade coaster with gold polka dots. Christina had gotten the house the coasters as a gift for doing well after our first week on campus.

"This is going to be the silliest talk we've ever had," I started. "I seriously can't believe I even went this far with it, but like I said, it's to stop this insane chatter."

Bri's eyes widened. "Ooh, but aren't we fans of insane chatter?"

"Not this kind," I said. "This insane chatter is driving me, well, *insane*."

"What's going on?" Bri asked. She mirrored me and set

her cup in front of her on a coaster. She tucked her legs under her.

"First, I wish I didn't have to say anything. You're my best friend, and I trust you like no one else. I don't want what I'm about to say to ruin your growing friendship with Clare."

Bri raised an eyebrow. "Um, okay."

"Clare's just looking out for me, but she's going to the extreme and sees something that's not there. She went to Khloe about it, and they both ganged up on me. Normally, I wouldn't cave to peer pressure. You know me."

Bri nodded. She didn't look worried at all. That made me feel even more confident that what I was about to say would be confirmed as a total misunderstanding.

"Clare said that she's noticed something 'off' with you lately. Like something's up and you're not telling us. She insisted it was true all weekend, and I told her that first, you're my bestie and you'd tell me, and second, I didn't see what she did. If anyone were to pick up on something 'off' with you, it would be me."

I picked up my mug and took a cautious sip of tea. It was the perfect temperature, and I took two more swallows before putting down the mug.

Brielle swallowed. But not tea.

"I just want Clare to stop looking for things, and that's why I asked you to meet me. I wanted to sit down, just you and me, and ask if there's anything going on that you haven't talked to me about or want to tell me. If not, I totally get it and Clare was wrong. I'll tell her we talked and there was nothing up with you, and then she'll back off."

Brielle's mouth opened, but no sound came out. "I—," she started. "Nothing is going on with me now."

Her words made me pause. "Why did you say 'now'?"

Brielle's face turned chalky white. She grabbed an orange pillow and clutched it across her stomach.

"Lauren," Brielle said.

"Bri, no." My voice was high. "I don't want Clare to be right. Everything okay, isn't it? You're not leaving Canterwood, are you?"

Brielle shook her head.

"Whew," I said. "That was my biggest fear. Talk to me. What's going on?"

Big tears filled Brielle's eyes. With one blink, they cascaded down her face and dripped onto the pillow.

"I've been keeping something from you," Brielle said. "Something really big. And Lauren, it started to make me feel *so* bad these past few days that I haven't been myself. Clare's right."

I froze. All I could do was stare at her.

Brielle swiped at her eyes. "I don't deserve to be crying. Lauren, please promise you'll listen to me and the whole story before you leave."

Slowly I nodded. I still couldn't speak. What was Brielle hiding that she couldn't tell *me* about?

"Lauren, I dated someone this past summer."

"You did? How? I was home for most of the summer."

"You were, but you were so busy looking for a horse and getting ready for Canterwood that you didn't have much time to hang out with Ana and me. It was the end of July when I started going out with this guy. We broke it off not too long ago."

"You don't have to be this upset that you dated someone and didn't tell me, Bri," I said. "I mean, I wish you would have told me, but like you said, I was busy. Still, you could always tell me anything."

There was a long pause.

Too long of a pause.

"Brielle? Who was the guy?" I asked. My heart thumped in my chest. Why was I afraid to hear the answer?

"Oh, Lauren. I wish I could take the whole thing back!

I can't believe I did it! I'm so sorry!" Brielle covered her face with her hands. Her shoulders shook, and I watched her struggle to regain composure.

"Laur, the guy I dated—" Brielle wiped at her tear-stained cheeks. "It was Taylor."

10

THOSE BETTER BE
FAKE TEARS

I SHOOK MY HEAD. "BRI, IF THIS IS A JOKE, it's not funny. I'm impressed that you mastered tears on command, but not for this."

"I wish it was a joke, Lauren." Brielle's voice was hoarse.

The entire room seemed to spin.

Clare had been right.

Khloe had been right.

Brielle had been keeping a secret.

Taylor had been keeping a secret.

Brielle had been my best friend.

Taylor had been my friend.

"It was after you guys broke up—I promise," Brielle said.

"As long as Taylor and I weren't together, that *so* makes it okay!" I interrupted.

Brielle fell silent. She hugged the couch pillow as if it was a shield from me. But nothing could hide this secret now. Brielle was completely exposed.

"Go on, please," I said, sweeping my hand in an encouraging gesture. "I want to hear every detail of this 'okay' story."

Brielle's posture was rigid. She looked as if I'd slapped her across the face. "I never said or thought it was okay. I knew better the entire time. At first it was the three of us going out a lot—Ana, Taylor, and me, or with some other people from school. One night Ana and I were supposed to meet Taylor to go to the movies, but Ana got sick. I went as his *friend* and, and, I don't know, I got caught up in it or something. We kept going out as a group, but after a while Taylor and I started going out on our own."

"Did he ask you? Or did you ask him?"

Brielle took a breath. "I asked him."

"Wow, Brielle. Wow." I picked up my mug, holding it so hard I worried for a second that I'd crack the ceramic.

"Lauren, there's no excuse. I knew I was breaking the best friend code by going out with your ex-boyfriend. But a tiny part of me rationalized it away by thinking about you here. You were in a new school, with new friends, new boys, a whole new life. You and Taylor were over."

"Like *you* just said, there's no excuse." I put down my mug without even taking a sip and crossed my arms. I'd never been so furious. Anger heated every part of my body, and my jaw was getting tired from being clenched.

"After the first time we went out, I was going to call you," Brielle said. Her eyes pleaded with me. But I felt nothing but anger. "I had my phone in my hand and put it down at the last second. I should have stopped things with Taylor then. If I couldn't tell you that I'd made a huge mistake and had gone on *one* date with him, that should have been a big enough warning sign to me to stop the relationship."

"Guess you missed the sign, huh, Brielle?" My tone got more and more biting with every word I said.

"I chose to ignore it." Opposite of my tone, Brielle's only got weaker. "I went out with him until he left for Canterwood. We both swore to each other that neither of us would ever tell you because it would only hurt you. Then he was gone."

"God, I'd almost forgotten that Taylor's been here lying to my face longer than you have," I said.

"We both did something so, so stupid, Lauren. I can't even begin to imagine how you feel right now. You can hate me if you want—you deserve to. Don't blame—"

"Don't you *dare* say not to blame Taylor," I interrupted. "He did this too. Not just you. I can and am blaming him. He wasn't innocent in any of this."

I quieted, trying to make sense of everything I'd just heard. Nothing made sense, though. This wasn't Brielle. My best friend from home would never do something like this to me. Neither would my ex-boyfriend.

A memory popped into my brain. "Wait. Wait. So what was that interaction between you guys in the parking lot on Family Day?"

Brielle looked at her lap for a few seconds. "Every word was a lie. It was a cover story that I made up on the fly. I actually went looking for Taylor, not my phone, and all he wanted to do was stay away from me and keep our pact intact. He saw me go right up to you and assumed I was about to tell you the truth. That's why he came after me."

Images of that day flashed in front of me. Taylor's angry face. Brielle shouting at him.

"I went over to him, and I guess I was hurt because he was ignoring me. It was the first time I'd seen him since we'd broken up. I wasn't going to go back on my word and tell you or try to get back together with him. I just wanted to say hi. But he was all freaked out, and I stressed out too."

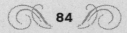

"You are an amazing liar," I said. "Congratulations. I bought your entire story that day. Every word. You should get together with Khloe and start taking acting classes."

I shook my head. This was the reason Taylor and Brielle hadn't been in the same room once since she'd gotten here. There had been so much going on that I hadn't had time to even address it. Every time a thought of saying something had started to form in my brain, something else happened. That was life at Canterwood.

"Do you know that I planned to talk to Taylor about how I thought he treated you that day?" I asked. "I would have looked so stupid! I was going to tell him that he couldn't speak to you like that and he needed to forgive you for the answering-machine mess. I was on *your* side. That was so dumb of me."

"You're not dumb. Please don't say that. I don't even know how to begin to apologize. I'm so beyond sorry, Lauren."

I wasn't up for this. Brielle knew better than to try to apologize right now for something of this magnitude.

I swiped my mug off the coffee table and stood. Without looking at Brielle, I dumped out my remaining tea, tossed the tea bag in the trash can, and walked out of the common room without a word.

II

BFF BETRAYAL

I FLUNG MY BEDROOM DOOR OPEN, SLAMMED it shut so hard that it rattled the photos on our wall, and dashed for my bed. Facedown, I fell into my pillow and the sobs racked my body.

"Lauren! Lauren! Omigod!" Khloe, whom I hadn't even seen in my haze, put a hand on my back. "Shhh. Lauren, it's okay. Whatever just happened, it's going to be all right. You and I will figure it out together." Khloe talked in a soothing tone over my pillow-muffled sobs. "There's nothing we can't get through. I promise, I'm here for you, sweetie."

Khloe stayed sitting on the edge of my bed and rubbed my back while I cried. With my eyes squeezed shut, all I could see were images of Taylor and Brielle together.

At his house.

At the movies.

At Yates.

Holding hands.

Smiling at each other with affection.

Kissing.

I pushed the images away, starting to hiccup. I couldn't breathe. It was too much. I'd never been betrayed like this before. Not by two people that I'd thought up until a few hours ago had cared about me.

"Can you sit up?" Khloe said quietly. "I'll get you a glass of water to help with the hiccups."

I let out a few more sobs and sat up. Khloe, still dressed in riding clothes, hurried to the mini-fridge to get me a bottle of water. She uncapped it, handing it to me.

"Thank you," I said, my voice raspy.

"Of course, LT." Khloe sat beside me again, quiet and not pressing me to talk.

That was one of the things I loved about her. Khloe had a larger-than-life personality that was going to take her straight to Broadway. But she also knew just when to take the BAM! I'M KHLOE!! down and be a calming presence.

I wiped my eyes and nose with the tissues Khloe had brought onto the bed. I stopped crying and drank some

water. Then tears started again, and I leaned onto Khloe's shoulder. She kept an arm around me, not saying a word.

I don't know how long we were like that. Just when I was sure I'd run out of tears, a fresh wave would hit and I'd be a snotty mess again. It had been a long while since my last crying spell now, and I didn't think I had another tear in me. My eyes felt dried up and my face tight.

I lifted my head from Khloe's shoulder and looked at her. She'd held me through all of this without an explanation. She deserved to know what was going on.

"Khloe," I said. "You were right."

She tilted her head. "About what?"

This part was harder. "*Clare* was right."

Khloe squeezed my shoulders. "Oh, Laur. Oh, no. I'm here to talk if you want, but *please* don't feel pressured."

"I don't," I said. "I really don't have any tears left." I barely recognized my own voice. It was emotionless.

"Okay." Khloe nodded. "I'm here."

"I didn't tell you because I swore that I was right, and I wanted to get my answers and then go to you and Clare. I met Brielle in the common room after our riding lesson. That's where I was before I came here." I took a shaky breath. "It's bad. Way worse than I could have ever imagined."

Anger flared pink in Khloe's cheeks. "Lauren, you know me. Just say the word and I'll go have a nice little 'talk' with Brielle."

I shook my head, closing my eyes. "None of us are talking to her. Khloe, she had a boyfriend at the end of summer. A boyfriend she didn't tell me about."

"What?" Khloe pursed her lips. "Why wouldn't she tell you? She's one of your best friends."

"I thought she was. Actually, I thought *two* people were. Her boyfriend? *Taylor*."

Khloe covered her mouth with her hand. Her eyes were round like an owl's, and she stared at me. "No. Way. No. Way. Why? Why would she do that to you?"

I shrugged. "She said she, Taylor, and Ana started hanging as a group, Ana had to miss a group date, and she and Taylor went together. Then magic. Less Ana, more the two of them."

"Taylor *never* hinted anything to you about this, right?" Khloe asked. "I mean, he wants you back!"

I laughed darkly. "Yep. He never said a word. Not one. He and Brielle made a 'pact' not to tell me, to spare my feelings. So lame. I'll tell you this long story later, but Brielle even lied to my face that day when she got in a screaming match with Taylor."

"Oh God." Khloe rubbed her forehead with her hand. "Since you just came from talking to Brielle, you obviously haven't talked to Taylor. What are you going to do about him?"

I picked up the mound of crumpled tissues around me. Getting up, I squeezed them hard in my fists before tossing them in our trash can.

"I'm going to wash my face and go find him. Right now. He's been walking around campus with this secret, and he's done. I'm sure Brielle already texted him, but I want to get to him before he has a chance to concoct some kind of apology in his head."

Khloe watched me as I turned on the hot water and smeared Neutrogena over my face.

"You sure you're okay, really okay, to talk to him?" she asked. "What you went through with Brielle was pretty traumatic, Laur. Do you want me to go with you or something?"

I rinsed my face and patted it with a hand towel. "You really are the best, Khlo. Thank you, but this is something I have to do on my own."

My phone beeped, and Khloe held it toward me.

"Can you check it?" I asked. "I don't want to see a message from Brielle right now."

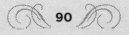

Khloe nodded, opening my BBM. "It's from Drew," she said. "He said, 'I'm ready to go to the media center now. Do you have an ETA? Can't wait to see you!'"

"Oh, shoot," I said. I took the phone from Khloe and sat back down next to her. "Drew asked me if I wanted to meet in the media center. He had to meet his swim coach, and I was planning on having what I thought would be a silly conversation with Brielle. Drew and I were going to do homework, then watch a movie."

"Maybe you should go meet him," Khloe said. "I could do a little light makeup, and your outfit is great."

I considered her suggestion. "I can't," I finally said. "I have to get this thing over with Taylor. If I see Drew, I'll be in a bad mood about it, and I don't want to drag Taylor baggage into our relationship."

"That makes sense," Khloe said.

I typed a message to Taylor first.

Lauren:

You free? Can we meet in the courtyard ASAP?

My urgency got his attention. Plus, we hadn't spoken in a while.

Taylor:

Yeah, just finished homework. I can b there in 5. Cool?

Lauren:

C u there.

Then I exited out of his name and went to Drew's.

Lauren:

Drew, I am SO sorry. I had 2 sit down & talk 2 Brielle. Things didn't go well, to put it lightly. I'm in an awful mood & now have 2 take care of something else.

I sent the message, knowing he was waiting for me.

Drew:

I'm sorry, Laur. Can I do anything?

Lauren:

You're sweet. I wish. Unfor, I have 2 do this myself.

Drew:

Totally understand. We'll take a rain check, OK?

Lauren:

You're the best. I promise, I'll explain everything 2 u when it's over. Things r just a mess right now.

Drew:

I'm giving u a giant hug from my dorm room. I'll b thinking abt u, Laur. Call, come over, BBM, whatever if u need me. I'm here 4 u.

Lauren:

I know u r. That's why I like u so much. Talk soon.

A lump formed in my throat. I knew my instinct would be to run to Drew after my conversation with Taylor. But I couldn't. Drew and Taylor had enough bad blood between them, and I couldn't add fuel to the fire. I had to wait until I was calm to tell Drew. Plus, I had Lex, Clare, and my other friends to rally around me.

I got up, stuck my phone in my pocket, and looked at Khloe.

She hadn't moved from my bed. KK stared at me with a soft expression. "Going?" she asked.

"Going."

Khloe stood, wrapping her arms around me in the tightest hug. "Take him down, LT. Do what you have to do."

Nodding, I slipped into my coat and cast a final look at her. "I will. The lies end today."

12

TRUTH TIME, TAYLOR

TAYLOR WAS ALREADY WAITING FOR ME WHEN I reached the courtyard. He was on his BlackBerry, but he looked up when my sneakers crunched a leaf on the sidewalk.

He smiled. "Hey, LT," he called.

I didn't answer.

As I walked toward him, I realized I couldn't tell anything was wrong. If I said nothing, if Brielle didn't tell him, Taylor and I could go on like *this*. With him giving me giant smiles, us running into each other in the hallways, me resisting fixing his collar, or noticing that he was wearing a new pair of jeans. Not noticing him in a boyfriend way, but a friend way. A *close* friend way. My "close" friend was just an illusion. Taylor wasn't that at all.

My chest swelled with anger the closer I got. Any

sadness I'd felt seconds ago was gone. He had lied to me, and I wanted to know why.

"Hey," I said, my tone short.

His green eyes, the ones I'd fallen for when we'd started dating, darted across my face.

"What's wrong?" he asked. "You've been crying."

"That's putting it mildly," I said, staring at him with my jaw set.

Taylor's lips parted a little. "Talk to me. Something happened. I'm sure I can help."

I didn't answer. I stood, my feet rooted to the cobble-stones. A cluster of laughing students passed behind me and I waited until they were down the sidewalk before opening my mouth.

"Actually, Taylor, *you* can't help."

I let the sentence hang in the air.

"You're the reason why I'm upset. The reason why I spent the past couple of hours crying. *You.* So thanks for your offer of 'help,' but I'll pass."

His head jerked back. "What are you talking about? Lauren, I didn't do—"

I couldn't hold it in for another second.

"Stop lying to me!" I screamed.

Taylor stepped back. Birds flew out of nearby trees,

and I wondered if a teacher was going to come looking for the source of the scream. I was too angry to care.

"Lying to you about *what*?" Taylor asked. His face was red, and he adjusted his gray beanie, pulling it tighter over his ears.

"Taylor Frost, I swear, if you make me tell you and you don't come clean, I'm *never* speaking to you again." I paused, my chest heaving. "You. Know. What. You. Did."

The red in his face slipped away. I was barely able to look at him as he stared into my eyes, not blinking or moving.

"Please," I said. It took everything I had to speak. My body already felt as though I'd run the New York City Marathon after my talk with Bri. Now I just wanted to crumple up in a ball. "If you care about me like you claim to, if you care even a *little*, just tell me."

"I dated Brielle this summer."

Taylor didn't hesitate. The words came out of his mouth, and by the look in his eyes and the twist of his mouth, I knew he hated himself right now. He had said the words, though, and the truth about our sort of lopsided dating triangle was out in the open.

"Thank you," I said. My voice was void of emotion. "That's all I wanted to hear."

I spun away from him, ignoring his calls after me.

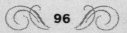

13

TWO FRIENDS GONE

I HUNCHED AGAINST THE COLD AS I WALKED to Hawthorne. I didn't need to stick around and hear Taylor's excuses about why he had dated my best friend. The simple truth from both of them was what I wanted. Now that I had it, there was no reason for me to be friends with either of them again.

Back in my room, I slid off my shoes and plopped into my desk chair. Khloe was at her desk, lamp on, doing homework. She put down her purple pen and spun her chair to face me.

"Um, did Taylor ditch you?" she asked. "That was awfully fast. Unless you've already disposed of his body and came back for my help concealing any and all evidence to save you from a life in an ugly orange jumpsuit behind bars."

I had to smile. Khloe was really trying to make me feel better.

"He's still breathing," I said. "He didn't bail. I asked him for the straight-up truth, and he gave it to me. One sentence was all I needed to hear. After that, I left."

"I don't know how you did that, but I'm proud of you," Khloe said, spinning her chair in a circle. "I would have pushed him into the fountain—still might on your behalf—or yelled at him until midnight."

I took my books from my bag and lined them up on my desk. "Believe me, it's not that I didn't want to do those things. I screamed at him a little before he would tell me. But I'm exhausted. There's no reason to ever talk to Taylor or Brielle again."

I opened my laptop and moved the wireless mouse to wake up the computer.

"You're totally done, huh?" Khloe asked.

"Forever and totally done."

"Good for you, Lauren. We're going to get you through this. I didn't text or call anyone while you were gone. I figured it's your business to tell people, and you can do that when you're ready."

"I have someone to talk to, and then I'll do homework to distract me," I said.

I pulled up instant messenger and logged on.

"Who are you talking to?" Khloe asked.

An icon was lit up, and the message "available" was next to her name.

"Ana," I said.

Khloe's eyes widened as she brought the tip of her pen to her mouth. "Oh, no. I forgot all about Ana. Do you think she . . . *knew?*"

"I don't know anything for sure anymore." I shook my head. "Everything I thought about two of the people closest to me was wrong. I'm not just going to assume Ana didn't know. I have to ask."

My palm sweated on the mouse. I hovered above Ana's icon. Ana wouldn't lie to me. I was either about to lose another best friend or keep one, all with one simple question.

Before I could chicken out, I double-clicked on Ana's name.

LaurBell:

Hi, Ana.

AnaArtiste:

*Laur! Hey! I'm so glad ur online! *does a dorky excited dance in her seat**

LaurBell:

Yeah, I had some time and I wanted to talk 2 u.

AnaArtiste:

scrambles 2 stay upright I almost fell off my chair. You have time? Whoa. Did the Canterwood science lab explode or did all of your teachers get the flu or something? U never have free time.

LaurBell:

Sci bldg is still standing last time I checked. And I have hmwk, but I really needed to talk to you.

AnaArtiste:

makes worried face Is something wrong?

I took a deep breath and wished a cup of Celestial Seasonings Tension Tamer tea would appear in front of me.

"Laur?"

I looked over my shoulder at Khloe. "Yeah?"

"I know you're super stressed right now. I can't do anything, but if you want, I *could* make you a cup of tea."

"Khloe Kinsella, I think we're psychically linked. I *just* thought about tea. That would be amazing. Thank you so much."

Khloe stood. "At your service, mademoiselle. What kind would you like?"

I told Khloe the tea I was craving, and she slipped out of the room. I turned back to my screen.

LaurBell:

Sorry I disappeared, A. Khloe just offered 2 make me tea.

AnaArtiste:

It's OK. What kind? That will tell me everything I need to know abt how ur feeling.

LaurBell:

Cel. Sea. Tension Tamer.

AnaArtiste:

Uh-oh. Okay. Breathe. What's up?

This was it. The next words Ana and I would exchange would change our friendship forever. Would a friendship even exist after our IM session ended? If Ana said she knew about Brielle and Taylor, I wasn't sure.

LaurBell:

4 the past couple of days, Brielle's roommate had been telling me that something was up w/B.

AnaArtiste:

Clare thought something was wrong? Like what?

LaurBell:

She didn't know 4 sure. Just felt like B was off.

AnaArtiste:

Did u hang out w/ B? Notice anything?

LaurBell:

Yeah, we had riding together & classes. Didn't pick up on anything.

AnaArtiste:

Hummm.

LaurBell:

Finally, I had 2 meet w Brielle and flat-out ask her if every-
thing was OK, bc Clare convinced Khloe that something was
wrong. . . .

AnaArtiste:

And let me guess . . . they both ganged up on you abt B.

LaurBell:

Exactly.

AnaArtiste:

What a rough spot to be in. I'm sorry, L. *hugs*

LaurBell:

It's much, much worse. Turns out, there was something V wrong
with Brielle.

I paused, my fingers hovering over the keys.

LaurBell:

Ana, I found out something abt Brielle. Do u have ANY idea
what I might be talking abt?

I watched the screen. Nothing. I dropped my head in
my hands as I waited for Ana to reply. Every passing second screamed that if Ana was going to say "no," it would
have already been on my screen.

AnaArtiste:

Lauren, I think this is a better phone conversation than IM. Can I call you?

She knew. Ana knew.

LaurBell:

Yeah. I'm here.

AnaArtiste:

Give me 5 mins 2 plug in my phone.

I pushed down my laptop lid as our doorknob twisted and Khloe walked into the room.

"Here you go," she said. "I added a few extra things just in case."

She slid a Tiffany-blue circle tray onto my desk. On a small plate next to my steaming mug of tea was an assortment of cookies—Milanos, coconut-flake-topped cookies, sugar cookies, and cookies with assorted jam in the middle.

"Khloe, did I mention that you are the definition of 'best friend'? Thank you so much." I smiled up at her and picked up the plate, offering her first pick at the cookies.

Khloe picked up a sugar cookie and bit into it. "I try," she said, smiling. "Plus, it's only fair that *I* make the tea sometimes. You always make it for us."

Her eyes swept across my desk and fell on my closed laptop.

"Everything okay with Ana?" Khloe asked, her tone soft.

"No," I said. "She's calling me any minute. She wouldn't answer me over IM. It's bad news."

Khloe reached over and squeezed my shoulder. "Whatever she says, Laur, remember all of the friends you have here. So many people care about you."

I picked up the GO CCA! mug and took a sip of the delicious tea. "I haven't forgotten for a second. You, Lex, and the rest of my friends are the only reason I'm not buried under a pile of blankets sobbing right now."

Riiing! Riiing!

I looked at my BlackBerry. A smiling Ana flashed on the screen.

Then I glanced back at Khloe.

Then back to my phone.

And again at my best friend.

"You've got this," Khloe said. "I'm right here."

Pressing my lips together, I picked up my phone and turned it on. "Hey," I said. I almost didn't recognize my own voice. It was chilly, raw from screaming, strained from crying, and tight from nerves.

"Hey," Ana said.

There was something wrong in her tone. She sounded scared and like she might start to cry at any second.

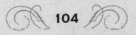

"Ana, I don't want to drag this out," I said. "I know your answer already. You knew about Taylor and Brielle, didn't you?"

"I . . . I am so sorry," Ana said in a whisper. "Oh my God, Lauren, I'm sorry. I didn't know what to do. I was trying to protect everyone and instead, I only ended up making things worse and hurting you."

"Ana, you don't have to explain. You chose Bri over me. Damage done."

With that, I hung up.

14

YOU *COULD* YELL "FIRE!"

MUCH LATER THAT NIGHT, ALL OF THE LIGHTS were off and Khloe and I were in bed. I ached for my sister Becca. I knew things would be a million times better if she were here. But I did have Khloe, who was no slob in the making-me-feel-better department.

"KK?" I asked. "You awake?"

"I'm up, Laur," Khloe said immediately. "What are you thinking about?"

"Everything," I said, shifting onto my back. "But mostly Ana right now. Why did she choose Brielle over me? I always thought we were equal best friends."

"I don't know," Khloe said. "Maybe Ana didn't want to hurt you. Maybe she thought Brielle would be able to keep what had happened a secret forever, and that way you wouldn't have to ever know."

"It makes me look so stupid," I said. "I share classes with Brielle and Taylor. I talked to each of them like nothing was wrong. That's because I didn't know! I believed that dumb lie Brielle told me about her 'fight' with Taylor."

Khloe rested her chin on her palm. "You know *you're* not dumb for believing Brielle, right? You thought your best friend was telling you the truth. You had no reason not to trust her."

"I still feel like I should have done something. Talked to Taylor. I planned to—to smooth things over between them. I just never got around to it. He's just as bad as Brielle. He came here, pretended to be my friend, and never told me about them."

"If Taylor had come to Canterwood and told you the truth right away, would you have forgiven him?" Khloe asked.

I hesitated. "I don't know. I think I would have gone easier on him. He had every opportunity to talk to me before Brielle got here. He could have told me since she arrived too."

"I bet he was scared. Plus, it's a hard thing to tell your

ex. I'm not defending him or anything. Just trying to understand, I guess."

"I don't know if I'll ever understand," I said. "Everything in my life was as close to perfect as possible. After one sit-down, Brielle and I are done, Taylor and I will never be friends, and I don't even know where to start with Ana."

"If I were you, I wouldn't rush to final decisions yet," Khloe said. "You're understandably hurt and furious. I think it would be better for you to make those decisions like 'I'm never talking to Brielle again' when you're less angry and can think a thousand percent straight."

I listened, staring up at the dark ceiling.

"At least that way, you'll know your decision came from your head and your heart and wasn't emotion ruled," Khloe added. "That's just my opinion."

"I'm definitely angry enough to want to BBM Ana, Brielle, and Taylor and tell them never to speak to me again." I let out a giant breath in a *whoosh*. "I do see your side. The last thing I want to have are regrets. Right now, I don't see any chance of me ever wanting to be their friend again, but I can't predict the future."

"That's my LT," Khloe said. "Focus on something else for a while. Stay busy. I'll help! But there's so much

going on, like prepping for the show, hanging out with your friends, spending time with Drew, getting ready for Thanksgiving break, and the million extra projects from teachers, that I don't think you'll even need my help."

"I am the queen of keeping busy," I said. "Thanks for talking to me, Khlo. I finally feel like I can sleep now."

"Of course, Laur. If I'm asleep and you want to talk, come over and shake me awake. I'm serious. You can even yell 'Fire!' to wake me."

I giggled. "What if Christina or someone else on our floor hears me saying that?"

"Hmm. Point. Maybe you better stick to 'Khloe!'"

I laughed and turned over, pressing my face into the pillow with a smile. Starting tomorrow, I was going to be the busiest student on the entire campus.

15

I'M SWITZERLAND

BEFORE CLASS THE NEXT MORNING, I BBMED
Clare.

Lauren:

Can u meet me in the common room 4 a sec?

She wrote back right away.

Clare:

Of course. BRT.

I shouldered my messenger bag and turned to Khloe,
who was buttoning her coat.

"I'm going to meet Clare for a minute and apologize,"
I said. "I owe it to her for not believing her about Brielle.
Or at least dismissing her claims so easily."

Khloe nodded. "I know Clare doesn't expect you to
apologize. That's really nice, Laur."

"It's the right thing to do. I'll see you in class."

With a wave to Khloe, I left the room.

I walked down Hawthorne's hallway and smiled at a few girls who shared classes with me. Light flowed out of Christina's office, and her voice was just audible. I loved this time of morning, when everyone was just waking up and the dorm hall was full of whispers as people got ready for class.

I walked into the common room, and the sitting area in front of the TV was empty, but Lexa and Jill, her roomie, were filling travel mugs with cappuccino from the machine. Clare wasn't here yet.

"Hey!" I said.

"Hi," Jill and Lexa said.

"You guys look *ultra*chic. Let me see those outfits!" I dropped my bag next to a chair and put my hands on my hips, looking my friends up and down.

Jill put down her mug. "Meee first!" She adjusted her Gucci black plastic-rimmed glasses and jutted out a hip.

I grabbed a wooden spoon from a rack and held it up to my mouth. "This morning," I said, pretending I was an entertainment news anchor, "we have Jill looking *amaze* in gray sweater tights, flat black booties with faux fur, and a ruffled black skirt."

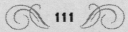

"Ooh! Click! Click!" Lexa, standing off to the side, mimed taking photographs.

Jill, grinning, twirled, her light-brown hair falling around her shoulders.

"And what's she wearing on top? She's chosen a fabulous peplum grape-colored top with a thick, chunky-knit oatmeal-colored sweater. Her outfit? Totally a ten!"

Lexa and I clapped, and Jill curtsied. Jill motioned for Lex to take her spot.

"We're lucky to have Lexa Reed now!" I said. "Let's dissect her fashion choices from head to toe."

Lexa smiled, putting a hand on her hip. She'd pulled her curly black hair with natural reddish highlights into a low bun.

"Lexa's sporting a school-appropriate yet oh-so-trendy tweed blazer with a white pima cotton shirt underneath."

Lexa switched hands and tilted her chin into the air.

"Lexa is keeping the look casual with a pair of dark skinny jeans tucked into dark-brown knee-high leather boots. Lexa's look gives her a total of ten points and ties her with Jill. It's a fashion win-win for two of Canterwood's most stunning fashionistas."

"Yay!" I cheered, clapping. We all laughed together.

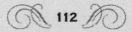

"Thanks for the morning pick-me-up, LT," Lexa said. She screwed the top onto her mug.

I turned on the teakettle on the stove. "Thank *you* guys for letting me play. You both really do look amazing."

Jill and Lex traded looks. They both turned, smiling at me.

"What?" I asked, laughing.

"It's your turn!"

Eagerly, I stepped onto the tiles where my friends had stood. Bright-red hair caught my eye. I looked over Lexa's shoulder, and Clare was walking across the common room toward us.

"Hey, Clare," I said.

My friends all greeted each other.

"Can we take a rain check on my turn?" I asked, looking at Lexa and Jill. "I need to talk to Clare before class."

Both girls nodded.

"Of course," Lexa said. "We've got to head out anyway. See you guys at lunch if not before!"

They took their coffee mugs and left. The teakettle whistled, and I took it off the burner.

"Thanks so much for meeting me before school," I said. This was going to be a little easier because I'd given

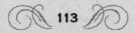

Khloe the green light to tell Clare about Bri's confession. At least I didn't have to recount the story.

Clare hopped up onto the counter and picked a green apple out of the fruit bowl. "Absolutely."

"Want any?" I motioned to the kettle.

Clare nodded, tucking a lock of long hair out of her eyes. "I'd *love* some of that energy-boosting green tea stuff you have. I can't remember the name of it."

I laughed. "That's okay. It's exactly what I'm having."

I handed Clare her tea, grabbed mine and a banana, and we went over to one of the couches. We settled on the same couch, both of us taking a bite of breakfast while our tea cooled on the coffee table.

"Clare," I said, "I owe you an apology."

Clare shook her head, opening her mouth. "Laur—"

"Please let me apologize?" I asked.

Clare closed her mouth and put her apple on a napkin on the table. "Go ahead."

"You're so cool that I know you don't think I owe you an 'I'm sorry.' But I do."

Clare gave me a tiny smile. Her blue eyes locked with mine.

"I didn't even give your claims about Brielle a fair chance. You're a really good friend, and I was so dumb.

I should have taken you seriously. I know you, and you wouldn't just pull something out of thin air and try to convince me that it's true."

Clare nodded, folding her hands on top of her jean-clad legs.

"Brielle was my best friend from home. I think part of me didn't want to hear you out because I didn't want to believe something was wrong or that Brielle was capable of keeping something like that from me. That doesn't make what I did okay. I'm only telling you what my thought process was."

"Lauren," Clare said. "You're right, first, that you don't owe me an apology. If anyone came to *me* and said Khloe was being weird but I hadn't noticed it, there's no way I would pay attention. I'd feel like I knew my best friend better than anyone, and if someone saw 'something,' then they were wrong."

"Exactly." I sipped my tea.

"Second, I understand not wanting to believe me. Like I just said, I really do. I'm not mad at you, and I'm not holding a grudge or anything. We're totally cool on my end."

"Thanks, Clare," I said, smiling.

"I'm really, really sorry that Brielle put you through this. Taylor, too."

"I know this puts you in an awkward position too," I said. "You share a room with Brielle, and you two have become friends in the short time she's been here. You *don't* have to tell me, but has she talked to you at all about this?"

"She has. Actually, Brielle said the same thing you just did. She apologized to me for making things weird now. She offered to try for a room transfer. I told her that wasn't necessary. I said that she and I were friends, what she did to you was *so* not okay and I was mad on your behalf, but I told Brielle that she could talk to me if she wanted. I knew she didn't have anyone else."

I was quiet for a few seconds while I took a couple of drinks of green tea. At first I'd bristled a bit when Clare had said she'd offered to stay friends with Brielle. This feeling swirled in my stomach, though.

"Honestly?" I said. "My first thought was 'What is Clare doing still offering friendship to Brielle?!'"

Clare nodded, twisting the diamond snowflake necklace at her throat. "I understand that. Completely."

"But the more I think about it, the more I'm glad you did. I can't be Brielle's friend right now. Maybe someday. Maybe never. I don't know yet. But we used to be so close, and the thought of her being at Canterwood with no one

upsets me. Even though I couldn't stomach the thought of us being friends."

Clare tilted her head. "That's really mature, Lauren. I don't know if I'd be able to do that. I promise I'm not about to put on a 'Team Brielle' T-shirt and forget what she did to you."

"Oh, I know you're not!" I said quickly.

"I'm just there if *she* prompts a conversation," Clare said. "That's it. I'm on your side with this, Laur, one thousand percent. But to keep the peace behind closed doors in my room, I'm kind of like Switzerland. You understand?"

"I get it, Clare," I said. "I would do the same in your position. I'd never want to be part of a problem that caused problems with you in your own space. That would make me feel so terrible. I appreciate your honesty about your feelings and everything with this situation. Thank you."

Clare leaned forward, an arm outstretched. We hugged, and both of us were smiling when we let go.

16

WHAT ATTENTION SPAN?

ALL DAY I FELT AS THOUGH I WAS HIDING from Taylor and Brielle. I kept my eyes down when I entered classes that we shared and almost ran from class to class. I knew Drew deserved to know what had happened, but I *hated* the idea of even telling him. He was going to be furious at Taylor and Brielle. I was more worried about Taylor, though, because they had swimming together and had to be around each other. Also, it didn't help that Taylor was my ex-boyfriend.

If I were in Drew's position, though, I would want to know what was going on. I hadn't been able to tell another person last night, and he'd understand that.

On my way to Hawthorne to change for my lesson, I pulled my phone out of my coat pocket.

I typed a BBM.

Lauren:

Hey, wanted 2 ask ahead of time . . . can u hang out w me 4 a while after riding? If u can, I want 2 tell u what happened yest.

Drew wrote me back before I'd reached the stable.

Drew:

Of course. We can go wherever u want 2 talk.

Lauren:

Thank u. C u in a few!

"Lauren!" Mr. Conner's voice had a hard edge to it.

I winced and looked at him. His arms were crossed where he stood, balanced on crutches, in the middle of the arena.

"I'm not going to ask any of you again—pay attention. I'm not here to waste my time. If you have something more important to do, please leave."

I bit down on my lip and kept my eyes between Whisper's ears. We were minutes away from the end of the lesson, thankfully. I'd messed up since Mr. Conner's first command to my group.

Before I'd entered the arena, I'd thought I'd prepared myself to share a relatively small space with Brielle. I hadn't seen her while I'd tacked up, and I'd warmed up

Whisper in the aisle and rode into the arena, pretending to have been there all along with everyone else, seconds before Mr. Conner entered.

It had only taken seconds for my eyes to shift from guiding Whisper to looking at Brielle. I stared at her, forgetting where I was for a minute, and she'd turned Zane as they made a figure eight. Her eyes connected with mine.

It had been the first exercise of class, and I accidentally jerked on Whisper's reins. She stepped out of the pattern we had been assigned and tossed her head. Mr. Conner had reprimanded me, and I'd spent the next few minutes fighting back embarrassed tears.

If I'd known how the lesson was going to go, I wouldn't have come. The first mistake had been far from my last. I kept getting distracted, and Whisper followed my lead. Mr. Conner's comments to me became sharper and sharper, but it was almost as if he was talking to someone else. I just couldn't get it together.

Now I felt sad and worn out. Whisper was annoyed with me. Her tail flicked from side to side, and she kept tugging the reins through my hands. I owed her a huge apology after the lesson. Normally, I would have been mortified if Mr. Conner had made *one* comment to me. But after six or seven, I'd kicked into a weird, numb kind

of state where I stopped absorbing his comments. All I could think about was Brielle. I didn't want every lesson from now on to be like this. She'd been called out on not paying attention too, and this wasn't good for Zane or Whisper.

Like a robot, I followed Mr. Conner's instructions to begin cooling out our horses. I let my eyes stay on Brielle's back. She had ended up directly in front of me. I knew Brielle well enough to know she felt bad. Her shoulders were slumped, and she was curled forward. Her leg positions were sloppy, and it was almost as if I could feel her vibes of sadness.

"I will see you tomorrow afternoon," Mr. Conner said. "Final warning: If you don't come to class prepared to concentrate and work, you'll be dismissed from class at the first sign of inattentive behavior."

He wasn't out of the arena for a half second before Brielle hopped off Zane's back and led him out of the arena. It only made me think about her more. I wondered if she was crying or upset with her performance. Or upset over us.

"Laur," a soft voice said.

I looked over, and Carina was beside me.

"Yeah?" I asked.

"C'mon. Let me help you cool Wisp down." It was then that I noticed Carina was on the ground holding Whisper's reins under the mare's chin.

"Lexa took Rocco," Carina explained. "I wanted to help you get Whisper back in her stall. Cool?"

I dismounted, tears making my vision blurry. This was Carina—a girl who jumped in wherever she could to help someone else. I'd seen her do it several times at the stable and in class. It was a quality I wanted to emulate.

"Thanks, Carina," I said in a whisper.

Together, Carina, Whisper, and I left the arena and that awful practice behind.

We made another pass down the aisle as we cooled down Whisper.

Carina patted Wisp's neck and looked over at me. "I think she's ready to be groomed. You?"

I reached up and ran a hand over Whisper, checking to make sure that she wasn't too warm.

"Agreed."

Carina and I were walking on opposite sides of Whisper, each of us holding a rein. During our walk, Carina had stayed mostly quiet, but offered up a few anec-dotes of moments during her trip from Sweden to the

US when she'd gotten lost or confused. They had been funny enough to keep my mind off my lesson. With each story, my mind had slowly refocused, and I'd shaken off the post-lesson haze that had clouded my vision.

I tugged on Whisper's rein, halting her.

Carina peered at me in front of Whisper.

"You okay?" she asked. Bits of her blond hair had escaped her long ponytail and hung around her ears and cheeks.

"Thanks to you," I said. "Carina, what you and Lex did for me—I can't thank you enough. I really let Mr. Conner get to me, and a problem that I'm dealing with sort of hit me when the lesson started. Really bad timing."

Carina gave me a sympathetic smile. "Oh, please. No thanks necessary. I've been *so* wanting to hang out with you more. We see each other here and there but rarely get a chance to hang out like this. I told Lex I'd owe her one if she cooled and groomed Rocco for me. But you know Lex—she'll never cash that in."

"She definitely won't," I said. "Lexa's awesome like that." I smiled at Carina. "But really, you've done more than enough. You should go—I can handle getting Whisper groomed and back in her stall. No arguments, either—I'm taking you to The Sweet Shoppe soon, my treat."

Carina grinned, her pink lips shiny with gloss. "Well, I *guess* I won't talk you out of The Sweet Shoppe. If it's okay, though, I'd like to hang with you while you finish up with Whisper. There's something I'd like to talk to you about."

"Of course I don't mind," I said. "You sit and relax, though. Deal?"

"Deal."

Carina walked over to join me on Whisper's left side, and I led my horse down the aisle. Carina and I waved at Lexa, who was chatting to Rocco as she groomed the gelding. Lex grinned at us and waved back, body brush in hand.

When we reached Whisper's stall, a clean Honor was munching hay from her hay net. "Cool with you if I groom Whisper inside her stall?" I asked Carina. Something told me she would appreciate the privacy of the stall walls when talking to me.

"Perfect," Carina said.

I led Whisper inside and changed her bridle for her halter. Carina got Whisper's tack box and set it in front of her stall.

I tied Whisper to the iron bars at the front of her stall and dug around in my box for the hoof pick.

"So, what's up?" I asked.

"Well, this is kind of something I wanted to tell you, Lexa, Cole, and the rest of my friends and teammates at once," Carina said. She leaned her back against Whisper's stall wall. "But timing hasn't worked out and I've got the opportunity to talk to you, so I want to take it."

"I'm honored that you want to share something with me," I said. "I feel like you and I have become friends faster than I thought was possible in the limited amount of time we've hung out."

"I feel the same," Carina said. She released her hair from its ponytail. "That's why I'm kind of afraid to talk to you more than anyone."

I bent over, picking Whisper's right hoof. I just *knew* Carina was going to tell me about her background. Unless she was going to blindside me with something totally new. But my gut said otherwise.

"Please don't be scared," I said. I scraped arena dirt from Whisper's hoof. "We're friends. You can talk to me."

I finished the hoof, stood, and looked at Carina. She looked nervous for the first time since we'd met. Her hands were shoved deep into the pocket of her down coat, she was shifting from boot to boot, and she played with the ends of her hair. Her ice-blue eyes were wide.

She took a big breath. "I want you to know who I am. The real Carina Johansson. When I found out I'd been accepted to Canterwood, I'd decided to keep my past from home to myself. I wanted you and the rest of the team to judge me on who I was *here*, not what I'd done at home."

I nodded.

"That was until I made friends. Plus, I just found out that if I want, I can apply to extend my stay at Canterwood."

"Oh, *mon Dieu!*" I exclaimed. "Carina! That's awesome! I know you're homesick, but you *have* to stay! Are you? Do you want to?"

Carina grinned. "I want to. I miss my family and my horses like *crazy*, and I don't know how I'm going to deal over Christmas, but I want to stay here. I love it so much."

"Yay!" I stepped forward, hugging her. Whisper, never one to miss a hug, nosed each of us with her muzzle.

We laughed, and I went back to Whisper's hind leg.

"That's not the news, but it's exciting," Carina said. "At home, in Sweden, I grew up on a horse farm. My parents met each other at a horse auction, and when they got married, they each combined their tiny start-up farms. It took years, but we've become a well-established stable in Sweden. Riders come from all over the country to buy

our Swedish Warmbloods, and we have a great trainer on staff—my trainer Aksel."

"Wow," I said, pretending it was the first time I'd heard about any of this. Carina had opened up to me on her own time, and I didn't want to make her feel bad.

"I've been competing in Sweden and Europe since I was a kid," she added. "I guess I have a good amount of experience." She paused, her fair face turning a little pink.

"What's a 'good amount'?" I asked. I picked Whisper's hoof and turned back to face Carina. I hoped if I prompted her with questions that it would make things easier on her.

"Um, well, right now, I'm currently the title holder of the Juniors' All Around Qualifier," Carina said. "It's nothing *huge*, but it's kind of important in my hometown."

"Wow," I said. "It doesn't sound small, Carina. That's so cool! I knew after watching you during all of our lessons that you were good. This isn't a surprise to me at all."

Carina smiled, looking down at her boots. "Thanks, Lauren. I didn't want you or anyone else to think I was hiding my riding experience. At the same time, I didn't want you to think I was telling you to brag about it. That's not my style. I hope you know that."

I rested a hand on Whisper's hindquarters. "I *do* know that. You're telling me about yourself, C, not bragging.

I want to know more about you. This title—those shows—that's you. Our friends will be just as excited as I am to learn about it—promise."

Carina's eyes quickly met mine. "Really? You think?"

"I *know*," I said. "Trust me. I've kind of got some experience in that department."

Carina raised an eyebrow. "Care to share?"

"If you can handle a sort of long story," I said, smiling.

"Hit me with it," Carina said.

As I groomed Whisper, I launched into my own coming-to-Canterwood story. The more I talked, the closer I felt to Carina and the stronger our friendship grew. Maybe the bad lesson had been a blessing in disguise.

17

HOT CHOCOLATE CURES EVERYTHING

"MMM. THANKS," I SAID, SMILING AT DREW. I had taken my first sip of the hot chocolate he'd gotten for me at The Sweet Shoppe. We'd walked over after Polo and Whisper had been tucked into their stalls for the evening.

"It's good," Drew agreed. He sipped his own cocoa. We had chosen a private table for two in the back of the Shoppe.

"I'm glad we came here. The smells and atmosphere always put me in a good mood," I said. I nodded toward my drink. "I definitely owe Carina one of those."

"She stayed with you until Whisper was cooled and groomed, right?" Drew asked.

Despite everything that had happened in class and what I was about to tell him, I couldn't help but notice how cute he looked. His black hair was a little tousled, and he wore a clover-green kangaroo-pocket hoodie that made his pale skin stand out.

"Carina helped with everything," I said. "Including talking me out of my bad mood after that lesson. She confided some info about herself with me, and it's something she's looking forward to sharing with you and the rest of our team."

"Can't wait to hear it," Drew said.

"I'm trying to tell myself that the bad lesson was worth it since Carina talked to me. But I wish I could permanently erase it from my brain."

"Everyone has a lesson like that. It happens. You'll wow Mr. Conner next time, and he'll forget all about it."

I smiled at Drew for trying to make me feel better. "I hope so." I took another sip of hot chocolate. "Enough about that lesson. Ugh. I'm glad you were able to meet me after riding so we could talk."

Drew's eyes settled on me. "Of course I'd meet you to talk. I'm guessing from the way you've acted today, it's something pretty bad."

"Bad to really, really bad."

Drew scooted his chair a little closer to mine. "I'm sorry."

"Me too." I sighed. "Over the weekend, Clare told me that something was up with Brielle."

"They're roommates, right?" Drew asked.

I nodded. "Clare couldn't tell me what exactly was going on because she didn't have proof of anything. She didn't hear Brielle on the phone or see an e-mail or anything that pointed to what was going on."

Drew was quiet, watching me. A couple of older students came into the Shoppe and stood at the counter. I crossed my fingers that no one from our grade would have a sweet tooth attack while Drew and I were here.

"I totally blew Clare off," I said. "She had no concrete proof, and I thought that since Bri was my best friend, if something *was* wrong, I'd see it before anyone else. But Clare wouldn't stop talking about it. Then she told Khloe, and you know how Khloe is about stuff like that. By yesterday morning, I knew I had to just ask Brielle if everything was cool so I could make Clare and Khlo see that I was right."

I took a long sip, and when I put down my cup, Drew's hand enclosed mine. Something about that sweet gesture gave me the courage to keep talking and get through this story for a final time.

"I met Brielle after riding. I'd planned to meet you

after we talked. I told Bri that I was meeting her for a silly reason and asked if anything was wrong. Turns out, she was hiding something from me and it had started to get to her."

"Oh, Laur." Drew's mouth turned down.

"Last summer and part of the fall, Brielle was dating someone. Ana knew and didn't tell me, and neither did Brielle."

Drew sat back in his chair a little.

"Brielle and the guy only stopped dating when he transferred schools."

I watched Drew, waiting for him to catch on. His expression was turning stony.

"He transferred to Canterwood."

Drew's jaw clenched so tight that I saw the muscles move in his face and chin.

"Then *she* transferred to Canterwood."

Drew's hands, resting on top of the table, balled into fists.

"And neither of them bothered to tell me about this incident. I found out when I questioned Brielle, not expecting to hear anything and only with the intent to silence Clare."

A string of inaudible words escaped from Drew's lips.

His cheeks turned scarlet, and he gripped the edge of the table with his hands, his fingertips turning white.

"Lauren. I don't know what to say." Drew's voice was deep and anger-filled.

"You don't have to say anything," I said. "Except that you, hopefully, don't want to break up with me because of yet another Taylor problem."

I swallowed, staring at him and awaiting his response.

"Oh, gosh, Lauren, no. Never!" Anger disappeared from his face and concern replaced it. He reached out a hand and I put mine in his.

"I was scared to tell you," I said. "I know how much it's put a strain on you to have Taylor here. It's not a normal situation. Plus, now you're both cocaptains on the swim team. You can't avoid him all the time. I'm so sorry."

Drew squeezed my hand. "Don't you ever apologize to me for this. You did nothing wrong. I'm glad you came to me and told me what happened. I'm *not* going to break up with you because of something someone else did. I can handle Taylor."

A breath that I'd been holding since I'd found out released. "I can't tell you how much better that makes me feel. I didn't want to lose you over this. I already talked to both of them, and I haven't spoken to them since."

"What do you want to happen next?" Drew asked. His cheeks slowly returned to their normal color. That gave me relief too. I didn't want him angry enough to get into a fight with Taylor or do anything that could get him into trouble.

I sighed. "I'm not sure. Right now, I can't imagine ever being friends with Brielle or Taylor again. Ana . . . I don't know. She was put in a bad spot. But Khloe and I talked a lot about this, and I don't want to make rash decisions that are emotion fueled. I need to take a step back from the whole thing for a while, stay away from Bri and Taylor, and see how it goes."

"That's one of the reasons why I like you so much," Drew said.

I smiled. "What do you mean?"

"You have *every* right to make Brielle's and Taylor's lives miserable here," Drew said. "But that's not you. You're bigger than that. You also don't write people off for one mistake."

"Well, like I said, I really don't see us ever being friends right *now*," I said. "But things change. I'm just going to focus on school, riding, and my friends." I grinned. "Oh, and *you*."

Drew smiled back, making me feel warm inside. "*That* is definitely the right decision."

18

DREW VS. TAYLOR

"I HATE THIS WEATHER," KHLOE GRUMBLED. She pulled her coat collar higher up around her neck. "If it's going to be this cold, at least make it worth it and *snow!*"

"Exactly what I said a few days ago," I said, hurrying up the sidewalk toward the English building. "This is brutal."

"I have to keep reminding myself that one day I'll be in sunny Los Angeles, and no temperature below sixty will touch my delicate skin."

"Have we discussed going to college in L.A. together?" I teased.

"Don't tempt me, LT," Khloe said, smiling through chattering teeth. "I might learn hypnotizing techniques and convince you that you want to live in L.A. with me because I can't be far away from my bestie."

"Aw, Khlo. That's sweet. Twisted. But sweet."

We laughed, leaning against each other. We stopped laughing at the same second when shouting rang across the campus.

". . . do that to her?"

". . . out of it."

I knew those voices. I glanced around, my heart pounding hard.

"There," Khloe said, pointing.

Next to the side of the math building, Drew and Taylor stared each other down. There was less than a foot of space between them, and Drew's posture was like I'd never seen before. It was aggressive and he leaned into Taylor, saying something I couldn't hear.

"Oh my God. They're going to get in trouble!"

I took off at a run, with Khloe right beside me. I clipped my shoulder against another student, but I was in too much of a hurry to apologize.

"Guys! Stop!" I called just as Khloe and I reached them.

Drew didn't move. His face was tight, and I felt the anger radiate off him. I glanced at Taylor, not having been this close to him since our fight. There was nothing but

defeat in his green eyes. I couldn't believe it when I felt a pang of sympathy for him.

"You didn't answer me," Drew said through clenched teeth. He didn't yell, but he may as well have—there was so much force behind his words. "How could you do this to her?"

Taylor's shoulders slumped. His body was thinner than usual, and he wasn't even wearing a coat.

"Drew," I started.

"I don't know," Taylor said, his tone quiet. He didn't look at Khloe or me. He kept his eyes on Drew. "It was the stupidest thing I've ever done."

Taylor fell silent and Drew stared at him, not moving.

My heartbeat pounded in my ears. There was *no* way Drew would actually punch Taylor, was there?

"You're both going to get in trouble," Khloe hissed. "Be quiet and leave each other alone. You're just making this worse for Lauren. And that's who you really care about, isn't it?"

Neither guy broke eye contact with the other.

"Isn't it?!" Khloe asked sharply and louder.

That broke their hold on each other. Drew stepped back, shaking his head. Taylor flicked his eyes downward and, with his head down, disappeared.

 **137**

Drew watched him go before looking at me. I searched his face and watched the anger vanish. *My* Drew reappeared.

"I'm sorry, Lauren," Drew said. He stuck his hands in his black coat pockets. "I didn't go looking for him. We honestly ran into each other, and I started it. He was going to keep walking, and I made the first move."

My teeth chattered from what had just happened—not the cold.

"Thank you for being honest," I said. "Please don't do that again. I don't want you to get in trouble, *and* I don't like you guys fighting. Please."

Drew reached out and touched my cheek. "I promise. I won't say another word to Taylor. I was a jerk."

"You better promise," Khloe said. Her tone was stern, and she was in total Protect the BFF mode. "Lauren's already been hurt enough. If *you* hurt her, remember that I know where you live."

Drew didn't make a joke out of Khloe's comment. He nodded at her. "I swear, Khloe. I would never hurt Lauren. You're a great friend for what you just did."

I looped my arm through Khloe's. "She's my best friend for a reason."

"We need to get to class," Khloe said. "C'mon, LT."

On sort-of-shaky legs, I moved a few steps with her.

"Laur?" Drew called.

I turned back toward his voice. In a few strides he was in front of me. He kissed my forehead lightly and ran a hand over my hair. "I'm sorry, again. I'll see you at lunch, if that's okay."

I nodded, smiling. "That's definitely okay."

19

BETTER
AND WORSE

THE DREW VS. TAYLOR THING ASIDE, THE rest of the day hadn't been as awkward as I'd feared. I ignored Brielle in the classes we shared, and she didn't try to approach me. I'd focused on classes and my friends. Somehow I'd managed to put this morning in the back of my brain and leave it there until I talked to Drew.

"I'm glad we're partners for the history project," Carina said.

"Me too!" I smiled at her.

We had bumped into each other on our way to lunch. Carina and I shared the same history class in second period, and we'd been paired up to write a research paper together.

"I'm still so new," Carina said, shifting her leather

messenger bag. "I was sweating thinking that anyone who got me as a partner would be like, 'Ugh. The new girl.'"

"No 'ugging' here." I made her smile. "I'm happy, because I've been around you enough in riding to know you're not going to bail on the project, leave me to do all of the work, and slap your name on it at the end."

"No way," Carina said. She shook her head. "I've had partners like that before at home. I'm good at history and science—those are my best subjects. My classmates know it too. So whenever we get to choose our partners, all of the slackers are suddenly my best friends. I try not to be rude, but I want to work with my friends or people who will actually, you know, *work*."

"I know all about that."

Together, we paused near a tall, leafy plant, making room for an older guy in a wheelchair to maneuver down the hall.

"Once," Carina said, gathering her long blond hair into a messy ponytail, "I had a science project that was worth half of my semester's grade. The teacher chose our partners, and I got stuck with the infamous and notoriously lazy Jon. He was *thrilled* that we were working together."

"Oh no," I said as we stepped back into the hallway.

We walked at a leisurely pace. I liked talking to Carina.

I wished I'd had more time to chat with her since she'd been here. Things had been busy, there had been drama, and I'd had my early issues with her. Once I had gotten to know her, though, she was one of the nicest people I'd ever met. She went out of her way to be kind, and she was genuinely excited about being here, aside from the occasional bout of homesickness. Carina fit in so well—both in classes and riding—it was as if she'd been a student here as long as I had.

"Big oh no," Carina continued. "Jon didn't even try. He came up to me when class had ended and said, 'I know how into this science stuff you are, so I'm going to do you a favor and be nice. The whole project is yours. Just don't forget to put my name on it. Have fun!'"

"Noooo way! Oh my God!" I whipped my head from side to side. "Are you *kidding* me? What kind of person does that? Jeez!"

"Jon truly believed that I wanted the entire project," Carina said. "I just stood there, staring after him, and thankfully, it was the last class of the day."

"What did you do?" I asked. "Please tell me you didn't do the whole thing yourself."

Carina looked at me and made an *oh, please* face. "Not at all. I did Jon a favor back."

I grinned, knowing whatever she was about to say was good. "I hate to interrupt," I said. "I want you to tell me the rest of the story, but I wanted to give you a heads-up that I promised to eat with Drew already. I didn't want to make you feel bad that we weren't going to sit together."

Carina shook her head. "No worries! You're lucky to have a cute boyfriend to eat with."

"Thanks, Carina. Okay, so tell me the 'favor' you did!"

We stepped into the caf. It was busy but not packed. Canterwood had things timed well right down to lunches. The cafeteria never felt overwhelmingly full of people, since we all had different lunch periods.

"Well, I had a good relationship with my science teacher. After I got home that day, I e-mailed him and explained what had happened. I didn't ask for a new partner. I did explain that unless Jon stepped up, it would be turned in with only my name."

"Your teacher talked to Jon, right?" I asked.

We got into the slow-moving lunch line. I smelled pizza—tasty thin-crust oven-baked—and lasagna. Both were *so* going on my plate.

"Not exactly. I got an e-mail back later, and my teacher thanked me for being honest and said he would handle the situation. He told me to reduce the project in half and do only that amount of work."

We picked up beige plastic trays.

"The next day I went to science, and toward the end of class, my teacher stood up and gave a short, casual speech about our projects. He reminded us that we'd be graded on *team* effort as well as the work we did, and if anyone did not participate, that person would get a zero."

"Ooh! Was that Jon's warning?" I asked. I used tongs to grab a clump of crisp romaine lettuce and put it on my tray.

"Yup." Carina laughed. "His *only* warning too! He didn't ask me once about how things were going, if I needed help—nothing. I turned in 'our' project, and he just assumed everything was fine."

"What a jerk," I said. I passed the salad tongs to Carina.

"Oh, he went down. Hard," Carina said. "A couple of weeks later we got our graded projects back. I got an A and Jon, sitting rows away from me, raised his hand and said he didn't get our papers back."

Suddenly I realized that I was so caught up in Carina's story that we'd sort of held up the lunch line. I made an *oops* face, and Carina looked over her shoulder. Her cheeks were pink when she looked back at me. We zipped our lips and focused on our salads.

I poured raspberry vinaigrette onto my lettuce and added feta cheese, dried cranberries, carrots, cucumbers, and candied walnuts. Carina used ranch dressing and added bright-colored peppers and tomatoes to her salad.

We moved on to the next lunch station. We gave our orders to the lunch lady and then had time to talk while we waited for our pizza and pasta.

"To end my rambling story," Carina said, "my teacher, without blinking, looked at Jon and told him that he hadn't turned in a project, so therefore he had no grade. Jon said he and I were partners—'we' must have forgotten to put his name on it."

I held out my tray for my food.

"That didn't work, did it?"

Carina shook her head. "Not a chance. My teacher said he'd warned everyone about teamwork and had seen none from Jon even during periods where my class had been told to pair up and work together. If Jon could use his laptop, produce the project, and send it to the classroom printer, then my teacher would take a look."

"Ohhh, Jon," I said, giggling.

"The entire class stared at him and watched his face go through about ten shades of red before turning purple. He finally mumbled that he couldn't find it on his computer. My teacher said then the grade stood."

"Sweet! Score for Carina!"

"And no more scoring for Jon," she said. She offered her tray to the lunch lady as I got mine back.

"What do you mean?"

"Jon got a zero, and his grade was already so low that it put him on academic probation. He was off the hockey team for the rest of the semester. Note that he was the star player."

My eyes widened. "Whoops. Bad play, Jon. Did he ever say anything to you?"

We headed for the drinks area and got plastic cups with lids and straws. I let Carina get ice first.

"He had plenty to say to me. After class, he found me and said that I'd set him up and I wasn't so smart after all for messing with him."

"Carina! That's bullying."

"I know," she said. She pressed the button for Dr Pepper. "He really got in my face, and our vice principal happened to walk by when Jon called me a nasty name. He got suspended for a week."

"Whoa." I watched my own cup fill with cherry Diet Coke. "Did he ever bother you again?"

"Nope. Never."

"Whew," I said as we stepped into the main caf room. "I'm sorry he attacked you, but I'm glad he got in trouble *and* left you alone after that."

Carina nodded. "Me too. I was worried, but I think Jon knew teachers were watching him."

We exchanged good-byes, and Carina headed toward Lexa, who waved her over. I spotted Drew at a table for two and walked over to him. I looked but didn't see Taylor anywhere. Or Brielle. At least lunch period was going to be drama free.

I put down my tray and sat across from Drew. He smiled when he saw me, but I saw the stress in his eyes.

"You feeling any better?" I asked.

My stomach did nervous flip-flops. I didn't want Drew to give up on us because my ex was causing problems at Canterwood.

"Better *and* worse," Drew said. He held out his hand across the table. I placed mine in his.

I squeezed his warm hand. "Why better and why worse?"

"Better because I got to say those things to someone who had hurt you," Drew said. "It felt so good to defend

you and let Taylor know how wrong he was. I wanted to make him hurt like he hurt you, even though I knew my words couldn't do it. But anything I could do to him in that moment felt like the right thing to do."

"Why worse?" I asked.

Drew looked down, then back at me. "Worse because how I acted with Taylor isn't me. You don't need me to defend you, Laur. I know you took care of things yourself. It was never my battle to fight unless you asked me to get involved. You didn't, and I jumped in."

Drew locked eyes with me. I rubbed my thumb across the top of his. I leaned closer to him.

"Drew, you did what you felt was right in the moment. You defended me. Stood up for me. I know that I didn't ask you to do anything, but it felt good to have someone do that for me." I gave him a tiny smile. "That's the selfish side of me. The other half of me stood there wishing you weren't fighting at all. I hated that you had been dragged into drama from my life and you were involved at all."

"So, we both feel better *and* worse, huh?" Drew asked.

I nodded. "Guess so."

"At least we feel the same way together." Drew leaned over the table and kissed my hand.

20

WHAT DAY IS IT, AGAIN?

DAYS MELTED TOGETHER, AND I MANAGED TO keep my life free of Brielle or Taylor interactions. I saw them in some classes, but I kept my eyes on the teacher or on my books. I hurried out of each class the second the bell rang, and I didn't hang around in the halls where I could run into either one of them.

When I had accidentally made eye contact with them, they each looked awful. Taylor looked as if he'd swum a dozen laps with his eyes open and the chlorine had irritated his eyes. Brielle looked just as tired and even more miserable. She never smiled, and both she and Taylor were silent during classes we shared.

My Canterwood friends had stepped up their support, and without them . . . I couldn't even imagine.

Whisper was probably ready to start charging me rent for being in her stall so much. Lexa had joked that Mr. Conner should add my name to Whisper's nameplate. She made me feel so calm, though, and was always there to listen. Plus, we were doing a lot of work. We had this weekend and next week left to practice. Then it was go time. During our last lesson, Mr. Conner had brought the sign-up sheet for the show. I'd decided on dressage and show jumping. I wanted to compete in one area where I felt comfortable and another that would challenge both Whisper and me.

I stayed busier than ever, intent on exhausting myself each day so when I went to bed, I'd fall asleep immediately. If I didn't, my thoughts wandered to Bri and Taylor.

When I thought about Brielle, memories flooded back to me. Memories from our time at Yates, the mall, watching movies, riding at Briar Creek, having sleepovers with Ana. I saw my smiling friend's face as she told a silly joke or listened to Ana or me share news. Even though I'd been at Canterwood and away from seeing Brielle daily, I'd gotten used to having her here in seconds. Brielle and I had fallen immediately back into our old groove, and she had fit right in with my Canterwood friends. As mad as I was, thinking about

Bri being sad made me feel bad. Same with Taylor. No matter what—I felt *awful*.

If I let myself think about Taylor, it was a different kind of hurt. He had been my boyfriend. We had shared so much with each other when we had been together. Taylor was the first boy who had ever made me feel pretty. The first guy I had wanted to dress up for. My first kiss. My first breakup.

When we had decided to break up last summer, it must have been one of the easiest splits in history. There had been a short period of awkwardness before we had transitioned into being friends. We'd maintained that friendship until and after I'd arrived at Canterwood. Sure, I hadn't known about his time with Brielle, but Taylor had his mind set on getting me back as his girlfriend. I'd never entertained the idea—my heart was with Drew— but I wanted Taylor in my life.

Now things would never be the same. Brielle's and Taylor's actions had caused them to be absent from my life. I was ducking Ana, too. She called and messaged me every day since we'd spoken on the phone, but I wasn't ready to talk to her. I just didn't know what to say.

I didn't know if I'd ever have the right words for Brielle or Taylor. Something kept nagging me, though—I

wasn't . . . *right* without them in my life. I had to find a way, somehow, to forgive them. I'd talked to my mom and Becca a lot over the past few days. They'd both been amazing listeners and gave me advice when I'd asked for it. They made it clear: They supported me no matter what I decided to do about Brielle, Taylor, and Ana.

One part that kept sticking in my mind was the upcoming holidays. I couldn't imagine them without my other three friends. The other night I'd been online after I'd finished homework. Khloe had been asleep, and I'd been on a Union message board that I used to visit often. My sisters and I used the forums during the holiday season to find a volunteer gig that we wanted to participate in. It was a family tradition—every year my parents, Becca, Charlotte, and I contributed to our community in some way during the holiday season. Once I'd met Ana, Brielle, and Taylor, we'd always done an activity together.

Volunteering during the holidays was a staple in my house. Both of my parents wanted my sisters and me to never forget how lucky and privileged we were and that so many families barely scraped by.

I'd found a thread asking for "Holiday Volunteer Elves!" and clicked on it to read the information. The thread had been started by the owner of a local

racehorse rehabilitation organization, Safe Haven for Thoroughbreds. This was the organization that all of my friends had donated to on my birthday. The charity took in injured Thoroughbreds who had been hurt during a race or training and were about to be sent to slaughter. SHT also adopted Thoroughbreds who weren't wanted for some reason or other by their owners—like racehorses who were at retirement age but the owners didn't want to care for the older horses.

SHT put the older horses out to pasture to let them live out their natural lives and spend their days grazing, playing, and enjoying their well-deserved retirement.

Younger horses or those recovered from an injury went through a retraining program with volunteers who had experience with ex-racehorses. The volunteers retrained the racehorses to become suitable pleasure horses. Once the rehabilitated horses were ready, SHT held adoption events and matched new owners to horses. I'd followed the organization on Chatter for years, but hadn't seen an open call for volunteers until now.

I reread the information and clicked onto SHT's website. This was *exactly* what I'd do for my holiday charity project. If I could recruit more volunteers . . . Carina! She popped into my mind immediately. We'd

talked about how she was sad to be spending Christmas at Canterwood alone. I'd already planned on asking Mom and Dad if she could come home with me. Now I had a fail-proof plan!

I copied the link, pasted it in an e-mail, and typed a quick message to Carina:

> *Hey!*
> *I was already planning to ask my parents if you could come home with me for Christmas. You interested? If so, what about helping me with this project? We'll talk about it tmrw!*
> *Xo*
> *~LT*

I sent the message, closed my laptop, and climbed under the covers. Hours must have passed before I finally drifted to sleep with a smile on my face. I'd concocted the *parfait* holiday plan. If I executed everything right, this Christmas was going to be like no other!

21

CALLING
A MEETING

ON FRIDAY AFTERNOON I SENT A MESSAGE TO
Taylor and Brielle.

Lauren:

*Taylor & Brielle, can u guys meet me in my room at 5? Taylor,
I'm getting permission from my dorm monitor for you to come inside.
It shouldn't be a problem.*

I watched my phone, chewing on the inside on my
cheek as I waited for a response.

My phone buzzed, and I picked it up.

Brielle:

I'll be there.

Taylor's name lit up too.

Taylor:

Of course. See you at five.

"Sent it," I said to Khloe. It was just after four, and we'd finished our riding lesson and had changed into comfy Friday night clothes—yoga pants and oversize sweaters. "They'll be here at five."

"Proud of you," Khlo said. She pulled on silver Puma slip-ons. "I'm heading out to meet Lex for a movie. I'll BBM you before I come back in case they're still here. I want to give you plenty of time to have a private convo."

"Thanks, KK. You're the best."

Once I'd talked to her about my plan, she'd immediately offered to go to the movies with a friend. I'd made it clear that she didn't have to leave—this was her room too. But Khloe had insisted.

We walked down the hallway together, and I waved as she headed out the door. I stood in Christina's doorjamb and knocked on her open door.

"Hi, Lauren," Christina said, smiling at me. She put down the pen she was holding and motioned for me to come inside. "What's new?"

"Not much," I said. I sank into a comfy chair on the opposite side of her desk. "Okay, actually a lot. I've had some big friendship problems recently."

Christina leaned back in her chair. "Oh, no. I'm so sorry to hear that."

"It got really bad, and I've been talking a lot to my other friends and my mom and sister."

"I'm glad you found people to talk to," Christina said. "Sometimes just talking it out can give you amazing perspective."

I nodded. "It did. That's why I'm here. I decided that I don't want to spend my time holding grudges and being angry at people. It's not just that—I miss them even though they did something horrible to me. I want to give them a second chance."

"That's an incredibly mature decision, Lauren," Christina said. "I'm extremely proud of you."

"Thank you. I came to ask a favor. I asked both of my friends to meet me in my room so we could talk. I wanted the most private place possible. Even Khloe went out for a movie so I'd have the room to myself."

Christina nodded.

"One of my friends is a guy . . . is it okay if he comes in my room and I shut the door?"

Christina rubbed her lips together. "Lauren, you know that's against Hawthorne's policy. No boys in dorm rooms, and *especially* not with the door shut."

I slumped in my seat.

"*But,*" Christina said, "I can tell this is serious and

you're not taking it lightly asking me. Your friends—both of them—may go into your room with the door shut. Just let me know when they leave, okay? If I knock on the door, I'll need you to answer, too."

"Oh, of course," I said. "Thank you so much, Christina. You have no idea how much I appreciate this. We're just going to be talking, I *promise*."

She smiled. "I believe you. Good luck with everything. You're a smart girl, and I know you'll find a way to work it out. Come talk to me if you need an ear, okay?"

"Okay. Thank you." I got up and left her office.

Back in my room, I shut the door and stared up at the wall clock. Half an hour. Thirty minutes. One thousand eight hundred seconds. If I didn't do something, I'd just stare at the clock until Brielle and Taylor got here.

I considered BBMing Drew, but I'd already told him about the plan. He'd been incredibly supportive. When I'd first explained, he'd been cautious—not wanting me to get hurt again by either Brielle or Taylor. I told him it was a risk that I was willing to take. It wasn't in my friends' nature to hurt people, especially friends, and I wanted to give them the benefit of the doubt that nothing like this would ever happen again.

It had been beyond difficult not to tell Drew about

my plan to volunteer with Safe Haven during Christmas break. It had been even harder not to tell him the new, bigger part of the plan that I'd thought of one night. But I had to wait. Things needed to be right with *all* of us before I talked to any of my friends about my holiday idea. Drew had asked me something exciting, though. He'd asked if I wanted to go out with him for Chinese food on Saturday night. I'd said *yes* in two seconds and was happy to have something fun to look forward to this weekend. The next weekend would be all business with the show.

Pushing up my sleeves, I pulled the vacuum out of the closet, made a mental list of all the things I could clean in half an hour, and got to work.

22

FORGIVENESS . . . POSSIBLE?

AT EXACTLY FIVE, NOT 4:59, OR 5:01, THERE was a knock at my door. Snippets of all the conversations I'd had with Mom, Khloe, Becca, Clare, Drew—everyone—ran through my head. They'd all helped me get here. Ultimately, it was up to me whether this invitation would be a failure or a success.

I put my hand on the doorknob. Flashes of Brielle, Taylor, Ana, me together raced through my head. I gripped the knob tighter and opened the door.

Brielle and Taylor stood apart from each other in the hallway. Brielle gave me the smile that said *I don't know if I'm supposed to smile or not*, and Taylor just stared at me.

Not one of us said a word.

Brielle shifted from one pink Converse to the other. She opened her mouth, then closed it.

"Hi."

Taylor's voice was quiet, low, but it seemed to reverberate off the hallway walls.

"Hey," Brielle said, following Taylor's lead. His one word seemed to have shattered the wall of silence that separated us all from each other. Taylor looked as if he'd put thought into his outfit—he had a long-sleeve red Ralph Lauren waffle-knit shirt under a wool-mix jacket. He wore clean dark-wash jeans and black Chucks.

"Hi," I said back. I looked at each of them before tilting my head to my door. "Want to come in? I think it's better than having our convo in the hallway."

They each nodded and followed me inside. I motioned to the love seat and chair near our coffee table.

"Feel free to sit wherever," I said, suddenly feeling nervous. Like I'd never had either of them in my home before. "Anyone want drinks?"

Brielle perched on the edge of the love seat, and Taylor did the same on the chair.

"Um," Brielle said. She fingered the ties on her yellow hoodie. I couldn't help but like her outfit. She'd paired the hoodie with light-gray yoga pants with a fold-over waistband. The band was rainbow-striped, and Brielle had worked a dozen tiny colored clips into her blond hair, which was secured in a half updo. I'd always told her that she looked great in any color.

"I'm having Diet Coke," I said, wondering if that would help.

"The same, please," Brielle said.

"Me too, please," Taylor said.

I got us all sodas, and they thanked me for them. Everything was so formal. So careful. As if a bomb would detonate if the wrong word was spoken or one of us did something out of line.

I opened my soda, Brielle and Taylor doing the same, and sat on the cushion next to Brielle. I turned so I could see both of them.

"I don't really know the right way to start this," I said. "So I'm just going to talk. I have a few things I want to say, and then I want to hear from both of you." I noticed how Taylor and Brielle wouldn't even look within arm's length of each other. "Before I start, I just want to say—you two *don't* have to purposely avoid each other in front of me. We all know what happened. By you trying not to look at each other, it only makes things more obvious. I want us all to try and remember how we used to act around each other."

Brielle and Taylor nodded. Taylor eased back into his seat a little. Brielle stopped picking at her nail polish.

"I didn't ask you guys here to start another inquisition. You've each already told me your side of the story, and that's enough for me. I responded to each of you in the moment and out of anger. Since some time has passed and I've had space to think, there are a few new things I'd like to say."

I clasped my hands together. "You guys were two of my best friends. I had different relationships with each of you, though they were equally important. When I found out I'd been accepted to Canterwood, some of my first thoughts were, 'What about Taylor and me?' and 'There's no way I'm leaving Brielle!' You were both a huge part of my life at a critical time for me. It was a time where I went through a lot of changes and leaned on both of you for support."

I took a breath, glancing between them. Both of their eyes were glued to me.

"If someone had told me three months ago that I'd be in a fight with each of you, I would have told that person he was nuts. What's hardest for me is *not* that you two were together, but that you kept it a secret, then lied about it and used Ana to help cover. If you'd come to me and

163

said, 'Hey, Lauren, we think we might want to go out, are you cool with that?' this whole thing never would have happened."

Brielle nodded hard.

"I'm over the fact that you went out with each other. You had every right to. I was a student at Canterwood, and I wasn't in a relationship with Taylor."

Taylor took a sip of his Diet Coke, and his green eyes looked back and forth between Brielle and me.

"Taylor, once you got here, I wish you'd told me. It would have been a hurdle that you and I would have to get over, but we would have. As *friends*. I need you to really, truly understand that I'm with Drew. You and I can't go back to the way things were."

Taylor cleared his throat. "I hear you. I apologize for continuing to push myself on you, Lauren. I should have been happy enough with the fact that we were friends."

"Thank you," I said.

I looked over at Brielle. "Bri, you started your time at Canterwood with a *giant* lie. But you came to Canterwood to get a fresh start, just like me, and I wish you'd trusted me enough to tell me the truth. It was a major breach of BFF code."

"I trust you with everything, Lauren," Brielle said.

"That was never it. I was furious with myself for what I'd done. I hoped I could keep it a secret, shoulder the blame with Taylor, and make sure you never found out. That was wrong. I'm so sorry."

I stared into my best friend's eyes, and I knew she meant it. We'd been friends long enough that I could read Brielle pretty well. Taylor, too. Neither of them seemed proud, like they'd almost gotten away with something. They seemed depressed.

"There's so much history among all of us," I continued. "At first I was willing to throw it all away because of this. But I talked to a lot of people and got some good advice. Finally, I followed my gut and called you here. I don't want our friendships to end. If you're in, let's take it slow and rebuild them. Learn to trust each other again. Be the Lauren and Taylor and Lauren and Brielle we used to be."

Their posture changed. Brielle and Taylor glanced back and forth at each other, then stared at me. Then back at each other again before both shaking their heads, eyes wide.

"Are you saying—," Brielle started, and stopped. She had an expression of *wanting* to be hopeful, but being afraid to be.

"I'm saying, I want you both to be my friends again. Life is too short for grudges, and everyone makes mistakes. I hope when it's my turn to mess up that you guys don't automatically cut me out of your lives."

"Oh, Lauren!"

Brielle was across the cushion in a flash. She wrapped her arms around me, and a few tears dripped onto my neck.

"I'm so, so sorry," Brielle said, sitting back as Taylor handed her a tissue from the coffee table. "I've missed you so much. I've been *miserable* without you. I promise my words aren't empty. I'll show you that you can trust me again."

I reached over and squeezed her hand. "I believe you. I love you, Bri."

"I love you, Laur."

At the same second, we both remembered Taylor. We glanced at him on his seat.

Ever so slowly, a wide grin spread across his face.

"Lauren Towers, I've never been sorrier than this. Not in my entire life. For you to have the capacity to forgive me and want to be my friend . . ." Taylor ran a hand over his hair. "I almost don't know what to say or do. I'm the happiest guy on campus right now. Like Brielle said, I

won't tell you all the ways I'm going to make it up to you. I'll show you. My life didn't feel complete without you in it."

We stood, and I darted around the coffee table, flinging my arms around Tay. His body was so familiar and his hug comforting.

"Three-way hug!" Brielle said after a minute. Taylor and I opened our arms and welcomed Brielle into our happy circle.

23

GOTTA BE A COINCIDENCE, RIGHT?

SATURDAY EVENING I STEPPED OUTSIDE OF Hawthorne's entrance door, where a smiling Drew waited, leaning against the iron railing. He looked as excited as I felt about going to Dragon Palace for Chinese food.

"You look beautiful," he said, his face lit up by the overhead lights.

Tonight was a few degrees warmer than normal, and I'd left my coat open to reveal my outfit. It had taken me hours to narrow down the possibilities from my closet. Then I'd recruited Khloe to help me narrow it down to three outfits and, finally, to one.

I'd decided on a sparkly light-and-dark-striped pink sweater with a ruffled black skirt. Under the skirt, I wore crisscross-pattern black tights with tall boots that went up to my knees. They were flat, so no worries of tripping. I'd accessorized with a Cartier knockoff bracelet that I'd found on eBay. It was silver and made to look like a nail that blacksmiths used to shoe horses. I carried a cross-body metallic silver purse just big enough to fit money, my cell phone, and student ID.

Khloe had picked out silver-and-pink dangly earrings. "It's Saturday night, LT," she'd said. "You're going to a place called 'Dragon Palace' for the first time with Drew. We've got to make sure your look slays the evil beast!"

The memory made me smile. After clothes and accessories, Khloe had done my makeup. Sheer champagne-colored eye shadow, Lip Buxom gloss from Sephora, a barely there dusting of powder across my T-zone, and a highlighting application of NARS blush on my cheekbones.

"I had a lot of help from Khloe," I said. "Thank you. You look great too."

Under an open wool coat, Drew wore a black V-neck sweater, jeans, and high-tops.

"Ready to go?" Drew asked, holding out a hand.

"Ready!"

After a brisk walk across campus, we walked inside the welcomed warm restaurant. Canterwood was adding new food places all the time, and Chinese was the latest. I had my fingers crossed for Indian next. The wide selection of food made me miss New York City a little less.

"Welcome to Dragon Palace," a waiter said. "Party of two?"

"Yes," Drew said.

"Follow me, please," the waiter answered.

I kept my eyes focused on Drew—it would be easy to lose him in here. Candles were lit along every wall, and the overhead lights had been dimmed low. We passed a waterfall with a koi pond, and I peered inside at the fish.

The smell of Chinese food made my mouth water, and I hoped Dragon Palace had speedy service!

The waiter seated Drew and me at a great table near an ascending row of candles along the wall.

"My name is Wei," the waiter said, smiling. "To start, what can I get you to drink?"

"Root beer would be great," I said. "Thank you."

"I'd love the same," Drew said. "Thanks."

Wei nodded and disappeared.

"This place is so cool!" I said. "Thank you for bringing me here."

Drew glanced around, nodding. Most of the tables were

filled, and waiters zipped around with food and drinks. "One question," Drew said. "Where's the dragon?"

"Ooh, yeah," I said. "Where is it?"

We both looked behind us, over each other's shoulders, toward the exit—everywhere.

"Uh, Laur," Drew said. "Look up."

I did as he said. A giant, intricate red-and-yellow dragon was painted on the ceiling. Smoke and fire blasted from his nose, and he was exactly the type of dragon I associated with the Chinese culture.

"Wow," I said. "That's gorgeous."

Drew didn't take his eyes off the ceiling. "It's amazing. Someone worked really, *really* hard on that."

I looked back down at the table, opening my menu. "It's been way too long since I've had Chinese food! Before I moved to Union, I ordered it at least once a week when I lived in Brooklyn. I've missed it so much at Canterwood." I scanned the menu. "They have *everything*! Ahhh! You're going to have to help me choose."

Drew looked at his own menu, playing with the corner. "Confession time," he said. "This is the first time I've ever had Chinese food."

"What?!" I slapped my hand over my mouth. "Drew, that was so rude. I didn't mean to make it worse. I was

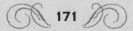

surprised because you seem like the kind of guy who's tried everything."

He smiled. "Everything except this Asian cuisine. Would you, um, help me order?"

"Of course! No big deal at all. Usually, when I get Chinese food with my friends, we split a couple of appetizers and then get bigger dishes to share. There's always so much food, and it's not too expensive, if you want to do that with me."

Drew nodded. "I'm game."

"For appetizers," I said, scanning the list, "I think you'd like a spring roll. When I suggest something, read over the description and say yes or no based on whether or not you like what's in it."

"Spring roll is a go," Drew said.

I reached back, grabbed a pen from my purse, and started writing down our order on my napkin.

"Another great dish is cold noodles with sesame sauce. The sauce is peanut buttery, and it doesn't sound the greatest from the description, but if we get it and you don't like it, then I would be shocked."

"Add it, please," Drew said.

Together, we went through the menu. We'd just finished when Wei appeared with our root beers.

"Ready to order?" he asked.

"Yes, please," I said. "Can we have two spring rolls, one cold noodles with sesame sauce, a small kung pao chicken with white rice, and an order of pork dumplings with extra soy sauce?"

Wei scratched down our order and read it back to us. "It'll be ready soon!" he said.

"Thank you, Lauren. I'm sorry I had to make you order and do all of the work."

"Stop," I said. "I was happy to do it, and I know you're going to do the same for me one day."

"So," Drew said, swirling his straw in his soda. "How did last night go?" He still looked a little embarrassed.

"Better than I could have hoped for," I said. "I really took to heart all the advice you and everyone else gave me about forgiveness and giving people second chances. Just because I told Brielle and Taylor we could be friends again does *not* mean I'm dropping my guard back to where it used to be."

"I think that's smart," Drew said. "I don't want you to get hurt."

"Me either. Until they both prove that I can trust them, my wall has to stay up. But I'm so, so happy, Drew, to have them back in my life. I missed them. I think I BBMed you that I called Ana, too, right?"

He nodded a *yes*. "I'm happy that Ana seemed to have learned a hard lesson but is so grateful to be your friend again. Honestly, from what you told me about these guys prior to this mess, I don't see any of them hurting you like this ever again. If they do"—Drew made a face like the Hulk and rubbed a clenched fist again an open palm—"it's on."

"I wanted to ask you something, and please be honest with me," I said. "Are you mad even the tiniest bit or bothered that I wanted Taylor back as my friend so bad?"

"Not for a second," Drew said, not even hesitating. "I know where your feelings lie, Lauren. You didn't want to befriend Taylor to win him back as your boyfriend. You did it because he *has* been a good friend to you for a long time. In this crazy world, I think we need all of the good friends we can get. I promise you that it doesn't bother me at all."

I beamed as Wei stepped up to our table carrying a huge tray of food. He placed it in front of us with speed and precision.

"Here are your chopsticks," Wei said. He reached into his apron and pulled out two plastic-wrapped pairs of wooden chopsticks. "Enjoy, and I'll be back to check on you."

"All right," I said. "Something else I get to teach you tonight! Chopsticks."

"A fork and knife are totally cool for me," Drew said.

"Nope." I leaned over and swiped his silverware off the table.

"Whoa, Towers," he said, laughing. "I guess it's chopsticks or my fingers then!"

"It's easier than you think, and it's fun. Plus, we're at the *Dragon Palace*. We've got to go all in here."

Drew looked up, then glanced down at me, his expression serious. "I think you're right. If we don't follow all ancient Chinese traditions"—he leaned closer to me—"we might release the dragon!" he said in a whisper.

I giggled. "Open your chopsticks. At least that'll give you a weapon if the dragon gets loose."

We unwrapped our plastic.

"Put one in each hand and rub them together like this," I said.

Drew watched me for a few seconds, then mimicked me.

"Perfect," I said. "Now, here's how you hold them."

I walked Drew through the demonstration three times before asking him to try. He came *so* close that I told him where to place his last finger.

"That's it!" I said. "Awesome job! Before you try

picking up food, try to grab something on the table. Use your fingers like this. . . ."

Drew's eyes followed my fingers. Within minutes, he tried using his chopsticks, and he'd picked up a napkin and napkin ring.

"You've got it," I said. "You're quite the student."

Drew smiled, looking at me in a way that made me feel like I was in a sauna. "I think you're quite the teacher."

We dug into our food, with me explaining a little about each dish and getting Drew's feedback once he'd tried it. I'd guessed right on everything we ordered, and there wasn't one thing Drew didn't like.

Wei came back, took our empty dishes, and handed each of us a fortune cookie.

Drew ripped the plastic off his as I set mine aside.

"Don't you want to read your fortune?" Drew asked.

I smiled. "I did all the time when I was a kid. But I've read them all by now. They say the same thing."

"Aw, c'mon, Laur. Read one more?"

I couldn't say no to him.

"What does yours say?" I asked as I unwrapped mine.

"'Love is for the lucky and the brave,'" he read.

I stopped fumbling with my wrapper, *very* aware of his eyes upon me. I looked up and our eyes locked. Drew's eyes were the blue I loved the most—the color of the ocean, clean, clear, and at its most beautiful.

"I've never heard that one before," I said, my voice a whisper.

"Maybe it wasn't time for you to hear it until now. Go on, open yours."

I cracked open my fortune cookie and tugged out the tiny slip of paper. I read the fortune. And read it again. And again. Wordlessly, I handed it to Drew.

"'There is a true and sincere friendship between you and your friends,'" he read aloud.

Our eyes met, and he placed the fortune in my palm, gently closing my hand over it.

"Never heard that one either?" Drew asked.

I shook my head.

"I think both of our fortunes are keepers."

I squeezed the paper in my hand, wanting more than anything to believe it was true, and watched Drew do the same with his paper.

Drew paid the bill and, holding hands, we left the restaurant. He stopped just down the sidewalk, letting go of my hand and sliding his around my waist.

"I wanted to do this at Dragon Palace," he said, his voice deep. "But I was afraid I'd release the dragon."

Kisskisskisskisskisskiss ran through my head. My brain went silent as we leaned into each other. I smelled the fresh-scented cologne he'd put on for tonight, and then our lips touched. Every single thing in my world disappeared, both the good and the bad. All I could feel—all I could process—was the slight pressure of Drew's soft lips touching mine and his hands holding me tight.

We pulled apart, and I felt dizzy.

"Wow," I said, whispering.

"Wow is right," he said back.

The gaslit lanterns lining the sidewalk cast soft shadows on his face.

"Drew, I want you to know that I've never felt like this before. Ever. You . . . do something to me, and kissing you or thinking about kissing you makes me dizzy! I get so nervous before every date and obsess over every detail, from what color hair band I'm going to use to what socks I want to wear."

Drew smiled.

"When we get together, though, you make me feel so comfortable. We fit together like we're old friends who will never run out of things to talk about. That makes me as happy as the thrill of kissing you."

Drew leaned forward and kissed my cheek. "That was

the sweetest, most amazing thing anyone's ever said to me, Lauren. I'll never forget it. I'm so glad I make you feel good, because you do all that and more for me. When I'm not with you, I'm thinking about ways we can be together. Then when we hang out, I go back and forth between trying to impress you and then forgetting and just having fun being myself."

Our breaths were visible in the night air, but I wasn't cold.

"You're my girl, LT."

I beamed, grabbed his hand, and tugged him forward, making him follow me as I skipped down the sidewalk, not caring how silly I looked. Our laughter rang over campus, and I knew this was a night that I'd never, ever forget.

24

THREE
FOR THREE

OVER THE NEXT FEW DAYS, LIFE SLOWLY,
very slowly, returned to normal. Brielle reintegrated herself
into my group of friends, and it was as if she'd never left.
Everyone was welcoming, and I couldn't have been happier to have her back. Part of me was still careful around
Bri, but most of me saw my old friend and hoped so hard
that one day our friendship would be completely back to
normal. Brielle's acceptance back in our group appeared to
lift stress off Clare, too. Each of us was happy. For those
of us on the intermediate team together, it translated to
our riding as well. Mr. Conner had commented on how
together we looked and how we were definitely ready for
the upcoming show.

It was then that I realized my group of friends was

so tight that our individual happiness depended on each other. If one of us was upset, it threw the entire group off balance. That realization had made me feel closer to my friends than ever, and I vowed to never take my friends for granted.

Taylor seemed to look better overnight after he'd met Brielle and me in my room. Color had returned to his face, and he didn't look sickly skinny or permanently disgusted with himself. We went back to sitting together in classes we shared and traded greetings when we passed each other in the hallway. Drew and I had passed Taylor in the lunchroom, and both guys managed polite hellos. I'd given Drew a giant hug and thanked him for being such a good boyfriend.

The night after my talk with Brielle and Taylor, I'd called Ana. Conversation had been a little stiff at first, but it didn't take long before we got comfortable with each other and I told Ana about my talk with Bri and Tay. I told her that Brielle had put Ana in a tough position, and when I tried to put myself in Ana's place, I didn't know what I would have done. If Ana had told me, she would have betrayed two friends. By staying silent, she was trying to keep one, me, safe and protect the secret of two, Brielle and Taylor. Ana had started crying and

apologizing. Whenever Ana cried, I cried. We had a teary sobfest and communicated how much we'd missed each other. By the end of the conversation, I had Ana-Banana back in my life. I was three for three.

Over those days, I thought more and more about my holiday idea and tried to work through any holes in the plan. It was going to take a Christmas miracle to pull it off, but I had belief in Santa this year.

With that thought in my head, I sent a mass e-mail:

> To: *Khloe Kinsella, Lexa Reed, Cole Harris,*
> *Drew Adams, Taylor Frost, Carina Johansson,*
> *Clare Bryant, Brielle Monaco, Zack Reynolds,*
> *Garret van Camp*
> From: *Lauren Towers*
> Subject: *A meeting of the minds on Thurs*
> *(tmrw)*
> *Hey, everyone!*
> *Sorry for the mass e-mail, but if I wrote you all*
> *individually . . . yeah.* ☺
> *This is kind of last-minute, but are you guys*
> *free to meet me in the Hawthorne common room*
> *tomorrow? I was thinking seven p.m., but the*
> *time is totally open for discussion. I kind of need*

you all there, so if seven doesn't work, e-mail me
back and we'll figure out a time that works for
everyone.
No, it's nothing bad! And no, not one of the
people that I invited knows what this meeting is
about! (Talking to YOU, Khloe Kinsella!)
E-mail me back when you can. I hope this works
for everyone!
xo,
~LT

I closed my computer, picked up my cell, and dialed a
very familiar number.

25

BEST PRESENT
EVER

CHRISTINA HAD OKAYED OUR GROUP MEET-
ing in Hawthorne's common room. As long as the door
was left open (she'd winked at me), and she had promised
to check on us. Lexa, Khloe, Clare, Brielle, and I all went
to the common room about fifteen minutes before everyone else was supposed to arrive at seven—the time agreed
upon by everyone.

"As hostesses," Khloe had said, "we have to make sure
the room is, as LT would say, *parfait.*"

Now everyone would start arriving any minute.

"I've got a huge teakettle of boiled water," I said to the
girls. "It'll stay hot for a long time in case anyone wants
tea, instant Starbucks coffee, or hot chocolate."

Bri, Clare, KK, and Lex nodded.

"Perf," Clare said.

"And I've got an assortment of teas laid out," I said, sweeping my arm over a basket. Nervous tingles shot through my stomach. I was about to propose something big—no, *huge*—and it could change e-v-e-r-y-t-h-i-n-g about Christmas break.

Everything.

"I set out some fruit from Harry and David," Clare said. "Pears, clementines, and apples. Plus, Bri helped me cut up cheese, and we've got cheddar, Monterey Jack, mozzarella, and cracked pepper."

Their cheese-and-cracker assortment looked mouth-watering.

"I did a soda check," Lexa said. "The fridge has everything. If we don't have it, it doesn't exist."

"Knock-knock!"

Our heads swiveled toward the voice at the doorjamb.

"Hey!" we all said, greeting Cole.

He stepped inside. Cole's light-brown hair was tousled, and he'd changed out of riding clothes and into dark-rinse jeans and a red cotton sweater.

"Sit anywhere," Khloe said. "Make yourself at home."

"Thanks," Cole said.

He sat on an armchair near the lit fireplace. We carried

over the food and tea basket, placing them on the coffee table between the two couches.

"I feel very important," Cole said, smiling. "It was like you *summoned* me here, Laur."

"And I feel very nervous," I said, trying to smile back. "This is the biggest idea I've ever had!"

Khloe flopped on one of the couches, pulling me down with her. She pouted. "And LT won't even tell *me*. Her best friend forever, who will be there at the very end at her bedside when she's dying."

"Khloe!" all of us cried out, making my roomie blush.

"Don't talk about my *death*!" I said. "Jeez!"

"I was just trying to make a point," Khloe said. She patted my arm. "Now you know that I'll be around forever."

"You can say that again," Lexa said, giggling.

Her infectious laughter made everyone, including me, laugh.

"Hey, guys!"

We turned and waved Carina into the room.

The lanky blonde walked across the room and sat next to Clare, who was on the couch with Lexa opposite Khloe, Brielle, and me.

"Thanks for inviting me to your dorm hall," Carina said. "Hawthorne is beautiful."

"Thanks for coming," I said. "I've visited your dorm before. Orchard's gorgeous too."

Within seconds, Drew, Zack, Taylor, and Garret all arrived and were seated on various couches or chairs. Bri and I had gotten drinks for everyone, and the cheese and crackers were disappearing.

"So," Zack said, peering around Khloe. The couple looked cozy sitting together. "What's up, LT?" He popped a Ritz cracker into his mouth.

I squeezed my fingers around my tea mug and traced the glittery blue snowflakes. What if no one wanted to come? Maybe this was the dumbest idea ever, and everyone would squirm and try to politely decline.

"Laur?" Drew, sitting on the couch's arm next to me, touched my shoulder.

"Sorry," I said. "I'm not going to lie, I'm nervous. This is either a crazy idea or a really good one."

"I like crazy," Khloe said. "Shoot."

Everyone stared at me.

I took a giant gulp of air. "Who wants to be an elf for Christmas?"

I got a room full of confused looks.

"I thought about Christmas break," I said. "I was online and saw that the retired racehorse charity in Union is looking for volunteers. They need people to groom the ex-racehorses, exercise them, and then there's a huge holiday adoption event. The dates work *perfectly* with our break from school."

I paused, looking at Drew. He smiled encouragingly.

"I called my parents and told them I wanted to volunteer. They thought it was great, and I asked . . . well, first I asked if Khloe, Lexa, Clare, and Carina could stay with us over break and volunteer too."

The girls grinned.

"Brielle already lives in Union," I added. "So maybe if you want to, Bri, we could have a few sleepovers at your house too. Maybe at Ana's too."

"Um, *yes!*" Bri said without pause. "I'm so in!"

Carina bobbed her head. "Lauren! This is so cool! I thought I'd be spending Christmas alone at Canterwood. I can't believe I have a chance to stay with you and actually spread some cheer during the holidays."

Khloe lightly socked my arm. "I'm *so* there! One problem: my parents. I don't know if they're going to say yes to me staying away from home for Christmas."

"Same with me," Clare said. "But I'm calling and asking."

"And we, the guys, come in *how*?" Cole asked.

My eyes flickered from boy to boy. "Actually, I already talked to Taylor about this idea last night. He's the only one who knew—sorry I said no one did, but I had to talk to Tay. I was too afraid of getting everyone excited only to find out the guys had nowhere to go. I talked to him because he's the only guy who lives in Union. I thought if any of you guys wanted to spend Christmas helping out, you could stay at Taylor's house. We just have to get Mr. and Mrs. Frost on board."

Taylor nodded. "That's not going to be easy. But I figure if I really, *really* focus on the volunteer part and make sure my dad knows it's something I can put on my transcript, he'll agree."

"Oh, cool," Zack said. He and Khloe traded grins and snuggled tighter on the couch.

They made me smile.

"I already know my parents will say yes," Garret said. "They spend every Christmas on a different tropical island, and I barely see them every holiday. I swear, a shark could have eaten me last year and they wouldn't have known. They won't miss me."

Garret looked down at his hands, like he'd regretted being so open.

"Hey, man," Taylor said. "It's *their* loss. My parents

don't travel for the holidays, but they may as well be in Tahiti. I don't spend time with them. I spent more time last year with our maid."

A look of understanding passed between the guys.

I never thought I'd be hearing anything like this. I'd been naive enough to think everyone would have a difficult time getting their parents to agree to the Union Holiday. Hearing Garret and Taylor talk made me sad. It only made me vow to throw the biggest, best Christmas bash for my friends and give them a holiday unlike anything they'd ever experienced.

"What about you?" I asked Drew. I looked up at him, staring in his blue eyes.

"My dad's going to be tough," Drew said. "But Laur, this is fantastic. I want to come."

"Put me down as a definite *yes*," Cole said. "Both of my parents are really big into charity on the holidays. I know without a doubt that they'll let me come."

"All right!" I said, smiling.

Everyone started talking at once about how they'd convince their parents.

"Guys," I said, interrupting, "I think the best way to convince your parents is to go the honest route. Obviously, Taylor will have to call his parents first. They'll have to

agree to host guests. Once that's done, maybe you can take turns calling your parents while you're here?"

Everyone nodded.

"Like I said, I think honesty is the way to go. You're not lying by saying you're doing something for charity—it's totally true. Your parents can look on the group's website and see the plea for volunteers. We'll be busy every single day, and it'll all culminate in the adopt-a-thon. If they're nervous about you staying with me or Taylor since they don't know us, my mom already said the girls' parents can call her."

I looked to Taylor. "So, Tay, if your parents agree, maybe your mom and dad can offer the same?"

He nodded. "Definitely."

"I can't wait another second," Khloe said. "I'm calling!"

"Me next!" Clare said, whipping out her BlackBerry.

We fell silent, trading grins, as Khloe dialed and put it on speakerphone.

"Hi, Mom!" she said into the phone when a woman answered after a few rings.

"Hi, hon. How are things?" Mrs. Kinsella asked.

"Everything's great. Really great, actually. I wanted to talk to you for a sec. Is Dad home?"

"He just got here," Mrs. Kinsella said.

"Can you put me on speakerphone?"

"Of course, honey. Hold on."

"Hey, Khlo," a man's voice said.

"Hi, Dad," KK said. "There's something I wanted to ask you both."

We stayed silent as Khloe explained the ex-racehorse event to her parents. She detailed what she'd be doing and where they could get more information, expressed how she'd miss her parents during Christmas but wouldn't ask unless it was important, and told them they could talk to my mom about it. Khloe's parents "mmmed" and "uhh-hed" as she spoke.

"What do you think?" Khloe finally asked.

My stomach flip-flopped. I wanted my bestie with me more than anything.

There was a pause. A *looong* pause. Oh, no. Mr. and Mrs. Kinsella were going to say—

"Khloe, sweetie," Mrs. Kinsella said. "Your dad and I love you so much and can't imagine Christmas without you. But we'll have to make do this year."

Ahhh!! I cheered in my head.

"We're proud of you, kiddo," Mr. Kinsella said. "You worked hard all year, and you're asking us permission to do something you love over your break. We'll call Lauren's mom to sort out details, but you may go. You're going to be the example of what Christmas is about."

"Thankyouthankyouthankyou!" Khloe squealed. "I'm going to miss you both too, so much. I've never been away for Christmas before, but I feel like I *have* to do this. Thank you so much for saying yes."

Khloe finished her phone call and pressed the end button with a triumphant smile.

"That's one down!" she cheered. "Put me down for a ride to Union!"

"Nice job, KK," I said. "I'm so excited!"

"My turn!" Clare said in a singsong voice.

Like Khloe, Clare put her phone on speaker. She twisted a red curl around her index finger as she told her parents a story close to Khloe's.

I kept my fingers crossed while we waited for Mr. and Mrs. Bryant's answer. Clare had the most trouble with her parents and even got an initial *no*, but Khloe had yelled into the phone that Clare had to come and help the horses or they wouldn't have a good Christmas.

Mr. and Mrs. Bryant, obviously used to Khloe's dramatics, had greeted her and laughed. They'd talked for a few more moments with Clare before finally giving her the go-ahead.

Brielle's battery was low, so she used my BlackBerry and called home. Mr. and Mrs. Monaco seemed excited about Bri's interest in volunteering over break. They added that as long as her end-of-semester grades were good, they would drive her to the stable any day she liked.

"Yes, yes, yes!" I said, standing and slapping palms with all of the girls. "Yay!"

We giggled together and raised our various glasses and mugs for a cheer.

"Now for the hard part," I said once we'd quieted down. "Convincing Taylor's parents to host the guys."

Taylor and I shared a look. We both knew the odds. I'd been his friend, then his girlfriend, long enough to know this wouldn't be an easy sell. If anything was going to derail my plan, it would be an instant no from Mr. Frosty Freeze.

Taylor cleared his throat and dialed. I barely breathed when his father answered in his crisp manner. Soon Taylor was explaining the situation to his parents. He took his time and was careful to not let it sound, well, like fun. He told a little white lie and said Mr. Conner had recommended that Taylor participate for the holidays and it would go a long way if he opened his home to other riders who wanted to help.

I swallowed. Hard. This was going to make or break it for the guys. I'd either spend Christmas with all my friends—*and* Drew—or it would be a girls' holiday. I didn't want to be away from Drew for Christmas. We were getting closer every day, and time apart sounded worse than getting coal in my Christmas stocking.

"Taylor," Mr. Frost said. "Your mother and I certainly are not open to the idea of hosting a party for you and all of your friends during Christmas."

Taylor started to open his mouth, but snapped it shut. He knew how to handle Mr. Frost.

"Dad," Taylor said, keeping his voice calm. There was no trace of frustration or annoyance in his tone. "I would never ask you or Mom to let me bring home my friends for Christmas. What I'm asking is for a place for riders from school to stay while we all participate in a volunteer program."

"Taylor, you don't even ride horses," Mrs. Frost said. "How did you get involved with this?"

It was the question I'd known was coming and had dreaded. Taylor's parents wanted him to have laserlike focus on school, a future in business, and swimming. Nothing else.

"I heard about it from a friend in my business elective,"

Taylor lied on the fly. "He said our teacher had told him that participating in a volunteer activity, especially over the holidays, would look great on my transcript. This is an organization recognized by Canterwood, so I'll probably get school credit for it."

Taylor took a breath. He looked at me. I nodded and mouthed *Go.*

"I looked at other organizations close to home, but there wasn't anything like this. It'll be good for me to broaden my transcript by working with horses."

"I'm glad you did your homework on this, Taylor," Mr. Frost said. "I certainly understand why a teacher would be impressed if you opened your home to like-minded students who want to volunteer."

"I may have even heard about this horse charity at the country club," Mrs..Frost said. "Horses are certainly an animal that I'd be pleased to have you familiar with."

This was sounding good. Taylor *had* lied, but they were lies for a good cause. I would have done the same.

"There will be rules, Taylor," Mr. Frost said. "This is not going to be a holiday for you to slack off and be out all day with your friends, sneaking off to the movies or the arcade."

"Of course not, sir," Taylor said.

"Your mother and I will discuss the ground rules with you later, but I approve of this idea. We are more than happy to do anything to further your education and better your future."

"Thank you, Dad," Taylor said. He kept his tone even. I knew why—if he acted too excited, then Mr. Frost would think he'd said yes to a party or something that might actually be fun for Taylor.

"I'll have Matilda begin to clean the guest rooms," Mrs. Frost said. "How many friends might we expect?"

"No more than four," Taylor said. "Is that all right?"

"We have plenty of rooms," Mrs. Frost said. "That's a perfectly acceptable number."

Like a dork, I danced in my seat, making Taylor look up at me and grin.

He stifled a laugh, thanked his parents, and hung up.

"Tay! Way to go!" I said. I hopped up off the couch and ran over to him, giving Taylor a one-armed hug.

"Thanks, Laur," Taylor said. His smile was huge.

"Everything was resting on *that* phone call," I said. "You were amazing."

Taylor waved his hand. "Please. C'mon, guys. Who's coming to my house?"

Drew held up his phone. "Let's find out."

Minutes later, we had Taylor's first guest confirmed as Drew hung up with a smile.

I reached up, and Drew took my hand. He squeezed it and smiled down at me.

"We get to spend Christmas together," he said. "How's that for a present?"

"Only the best one I can imagine," I said. "Only the best."

As the rest of the guys called, my pile of "presents" kept piling up as each and every set of parents said yes.

26

TOMORROW'S
THE DAY

ON FRIDAY AFTERNOON, I WALKED TO THE
indoor arena without Whisper. Mr. Conner had sent my
class an e-mail, instructing us to come without our horses.
I stood next to Carina and Cole. Soon the rest of our class
trickled in. At the exact *second* class began, Mr. Conner
entered the room. He moved quickly on his crutches and
stood before us.

"Good afternoon," he said.

"Good afternoon, Mr. Conner," we said back.

"As I'm sure you're well aware," Mr. Conner started,
"tomorrow is a big day. You'll be closing out the show year
and ending on what I hope will be a positive note. Visiting
schools will be here as both guests and competition. As
the host of the final show of the season, I want each of

you to be well rested, have both yourself and your horse prepared, and be ready to welcome our guests."

I couldn't believe it was the last show of the year. It felt as though Whisper and I had just gotten started. That was true in a way, since we were a fairly new pair. I wanted to do well in my classes and end the year on a high note. Both for myself and for Whisper.

"We won't be riding this afternoon," Mr. Conner said. "Instead I'm giving you this session off. Please use your time *wisely*." The instructor eyed each of us. "Tomorrow, I want tack spotless, horses that are well groomed, manes and tails that are braided, and for you to look your very best."

I started making a mental list of all the things I had to do. *Braids, tack, pick out show clothes . . .*

"Please use this time to prepare for tomorrow," Mr. Conner said. "I do not want to see anyone not ready tomorrow. If your turnout is not spotless, you will not be participating. With this free period, I'm giving you adequate time to prepare for tomorrow. Nothing less than perfect will be accepted, and excuses will not be tolerated."

I shrank back on my heels a little at his words. I'd stay all night if I had to—anything to avoid Mr. Conner's wrath *and* missing the show.

Mr. Conner smiled. "With that said, I want tomorrow to be fun as well as a learning experience. I'm proud to have each of you representing Canterwood Crest Academy and me. I have no doubt that you'll each do a fine job."

I shifted my eyes to Carina, and we traded little smiles.

"Now, I won't take up any more of your time. You're free to go, and I will see you bright and early. Come and find me or Mike or Doug if you have any questions in the meantime."

Mr. Conner dipped his head to us and exited the arena. Once he stepped out of the riding space, chatter erupted as we clustered together.

"I've got *so* much to do," Brielle said. "You guys?"

"My tack's a teensy bit dirty," Khloe said, holding up her hand and using her thumb and index finger to illustrate her point.

"Mine too," Cole said. "I haven't even started braiding Valentino yet."

"I've got braids to do. My tack isn't bad, but I've got to wipe it down," I said.

Lexa, Carina, and Drew chimed in with their to-do items.

"I don't know about you guys," Drew said. "But I'm going to make sure Polo is perfectly clean and so is his

tack. I definitely don't want to be barred from competing tomorrow."

"Me either!" I said.

The rest of my teammates shook their heads in agreement. With that, we semi-dashed for the arena exit, and show preparation began.

In the tack room, I sorted through the box of braiding supplies. The door opened and Drew stepped inside.

"Hey," he said. "What are you working on?"

"Braids, then tack," I said. "You?"

"Same. Want to find a quiet spot somewhere and do our braids together?"

He took a step closer to me. Close enough so I could smell his cinnamon-scented breath.

I clutched the plastic bin. "Yes," I said, almost unable to breathe.

"I can't wait to spend Christmas with you," Drew said.

I glanced from his lips to his eyes. Drew's eyes said everything about him. I could tell his mood based on the color of his eyes. Right now, they were a stunning ocean blue.

"Me either," I said.

Drew took another step, and the bin was pressed between our chests.

202

"Just in case," Drew said, "I'm bringing a suitcase full of mistletoe."

I couldn't find words to show him how happy that made me. Instead I leaned forward and touched my lips to his. It felt like it did the first time we had kissed—electricity jolted through my body, and now I *truly* felt breathless. We parted, opening our eyes and staring at each other for seconds—no one speaking. No words needed to be said.

27

NEW MANDATE

Polo and Whisper down the aisle as we looked for a quiet spot.

"Ooh, how about here?" I suggested.

Two tie rings near the empty hot walker were free.

"Let's snag those rings," Drew said.

We tied Polo and Whisper to the tie rings. I tied Whisper's head close to the ring. I couldn't give her much lead line, because I needed her extra still for braiding.

I put my caddy of supplies I'd brought for Drew and me on a low shelf in between us. I rummaged through the left side of the caddy, where I'd put my supplies. Drew's were on the right. I picked out a comb and handful of clothespins.

Taking my time, I combed Whisper's long mane. I'd pulled her mane a few days ago, so it was even in length and thickness.

Using the comb, I sectioned off Whisper's mane into fifteen pieces. I clipped each piece with a wooden clothespin to keep my sections separated.

"Okay, girl," I said. "Time for a little water. Just a tiny bit."

Whisper eyed the purple spray bottle that I took from the caddy. I kept the nozzle pointed away from her face as I spritzed her mane until each section was damp.

I put the spray bottle back and took out a gray ball of yarn and a pair of scissors. For each section, I cut two pieces of yarn that were identical in length. Mr. Conner had every color of yarn imaginable in the tack room, and I'd found the ideal match for Whisper—the yarn was going to blend seamlessly into her mane and tail.

I laid my pairs of yarn across my side of the caddy. Once I had enough, I picked up two pieces and started the first braid closest to Whisper's poll. I took my time, doing a tight braid and working in both pieces of yarn. At the end of the braid, I tied a slip knot. I moved down Whisper's mane, doing the same to each section.

Drew worked in comfortable silence next to us. Polo

was the perfect companion for Whisper. The quarter horse gelding was calm and relaxed, already starting to doze off.

Finally I'd finished all the braids, and they hung down in a neat row. I plucked the pull-through from the caddy. It was mine that I'd had *forever*. I'd made it with a piece of wire from one of Kim's hay bales. I'd twisted the wire, leaving a circle about the size of a dime at the end, and a handle that I'd covered in black tape. I looked at it, smiling. Ana and Brielle had bought their pull-throughs at a Union craft store. Once Brielle had seen mine, she'd retired hers and begged me to show her how to make one like mine.

Ready to turn the braid into a rosette, I tied the first braid into a tight knot with the yarn and then used the pull-through to bring the yarn through to the top of the braid. I secured the button-shaped braid by running the yarn under the rosette and back to the top, tying it tight with two knots. Now I had to repeat the process fourteen times.

After all of the braids were turned into button braids, I used scissors to trim the extra yarn.

Footsteps shuffled in my direction, and Drew peeked around Whisper's neck. She snuggled her muzzle into Drew's shoulder. I smiled—my horse had *excellent* taste.

"I just wanted to see how pathetic my braids look compared to yours," Drew said. He was doing button braids too, even though he wasn't taking a dressage class.

"Oh, stop," I said. I shook my head. "I'm sure yours are great."

Drew walked around Whisper, patting her chest, and looked at my handiwork.

"Wow." He nodded. "Yep, I was right."

"Drew!"

I patted Whisper's rump as I walked behind her and over to Polo's left side. Drew hadn't finished yet, but his braids were round and tied tight. Some were a little bigger than others, but you had to be looking for flaws to notice.

"You're nuts," I declared. "They look great."

Drew and I swapped sides, going back to our horses. "I'm glad I didn't cut my yarn," he said. "I never tie a second knot. Now I am."

"I didn't tie two knots for a long time," I said. "I started to after I worked for hours on braiding this horse's mane for a really big show. Overnight, he rubbed them up against the stall wall and when I walked in, ready to take him to the trailer, I found *all* but two of my button braids undone."

"Ouch," Drew said.

"I cried," I admitted. "My instructor told me I was lucky and there was time to fix them at the show grounds, but he chastised me for not double knotting."

"Aw, I don't like to think about you crying," Drew said.

"I don't like to think about braids coming undone overnight."

Smiling into Whisper's coat, I leaned my head against her shoulder. Working beside Drew had a calming effect on me. Usually I prepped for a show by myself. It was nice to have company for a change. Polo seemed to have the same effect on Whisper. She'd never been so still during a braiding session before. Maybe prepping with Drew was a new, *mandatory* part of my show prep.

28

OUT WITH
A BANG

FRIDAY NIGHT I'D SWAPPED MY USUAL TEA for Diet Coke as Khloe and I packed for Thanksgiving break *and* chose our clothes for tomorrow's show at the same time. I was exhausted from the week, and even though I'd had two cups of green tea, it wasn't enough caffeine to keep me going.

"I can't believe tomorrow's our last competition of the year," I said. "Can you?"

Khloe, arms full of clothes of every color, shook her head. "Feels like we just got started."

"I'm excited about Thanksgiving, but I'm *really* pumped about Christmas. I can't believe you, Lex, Clare, and the rest of our friends are all spending the holiday in Union!"

Khloe dropped her clothes on her bed, clasping her

hands. "Omigod! I know! I seriously owe my parents for saying yes. I was sure they'd be all, 'No way are you missing a family holiday.' But they knew how important the charity is to me."

"Mine too," I said. "The *biggest* shocker of all is Taylor. He's not even on the riding team and his dad agreed to let Drew, Cole, Zack, and Garret stay at their house. Taylor's psyched. He never gets to have friends over. Like, ever. Bri, Ana, and I dubbed his parents 'the Frosty Freezes' for a reason."

Khloe walked around her bed to her nightstand. "I think," she said, "this calls for a little music to put us in the mood."

Soon "Jingle Bells" burst through her iPod speakers.

"Brill!" I said. "Exactly what we needed."

I folded another sweater, a pink Ralph Lauren cable knit with a green pony stitched on, and put it in my duffel bag. I wasn't taking much home for Thanksgiving. The break wasn't going to be long.

A knock at the door came while "Rockin' Around the Christmas Tree" played. Khloe, closest, walked over and opened it. Brielle, twirling a lock of blond hair around her finger, smiled at Khloe and peeked over KK's shoulder to smile at me.

"Hey, guys," Bri said. "Mind if I come in for a sec?"

"C'mon in," I said.

Khloe held open the door for Bri and my friend stepped inside, shutting the door behind her.

"Love the music," Brielle said. "Ahhh, I can already smell that Christmas tree scent."

"I can't wait," I said.

"Make a seat for yourself anywhere you can," Khloe told Bri. "Move any of my clothes. There's no order system. Unlike LT's."

"Yeah," I said, pretending to sound serious. "Don't move my piles coordinated by color and fabric."

We all laughed.

"So, what's up?" I asked Bri. Now that we'd made up over the Taylor thing, it was good to have my old friend back. I didn't know if things would ever be the same, but it felt right to at least try. And Bri was making up for it in every way she could. She was there whenever I needed her, and I saw the effort she was making to prove herself to me.

"I had to talk to someone about the show," Brielle said. "Clare's out and I was going stir-crazy in our room. I have no clue what the drill is around here. Fill me in?"

"Sure," I said. KK nodded.

"Get up at four thirty," I said. "Even though we're showing here, you'll want the extra time. As soon as you're dressed—and don't forget a long hoodie to cover your show clothes—head down to the stable. Riders usually start arriving by six."

"I usually keep Ever in her stall since there's so much commotion outside," Khloe said. "Or I'll use a tie ring in the back of the stable or crossties that are away from everyone else."

"Good idea," Brielle said. "Zane should be used to the noise after being a stable horse for a while, but I def want to minimize any possible stress on him."

"After that, it's pretty much the same as it was at Briar Creek," I said. "Tack up, warm up in one of the big arenas, and be sure to listen for the loudspeaker to announce your class."

"I didn't even ask," Khlo said. She stuffed a pile of something pink into her duffel bag. "What are you taking?"

"Intermediate equitation and intermediate cross-country," Brielle said. "I want to get one last cross-country ride in before the snow and the ground gets too hard."

"Cool," Khloe said. "I'm doing advanced dressage and advanced equitation."

 212

"You're doing intermediate show jumping and intermediate dressage, right?" Brielle asked me.

"Yeah. I want to face down my jumping phobia at the end of the year."

Both girls nodded. Brielle held a pile of Khloe's PINK pj's on her lap while she sat on KK's desk chair.

"That's a big deal, LT," Khloe said. She turned to smile at me. The pink rhinestone-heart bobby pin in her hair sparkled.

"I want to just do it," I said. I grabbed my last sweater—a yellow V-neck Mom and Dad had gotten me for winter. "I could have taken another class, and Mr. Conner didn't pressure me to take a jumping class, but I want to. Hopefully, I'll do well, and it'll boost my self-esteem and Whisper's."

"You'll be awesome!" Khloe and Bri exclaimed at the same time.

The three of us burst into giggles, and I couldn't have been happier than to have the support of my friends.

29

A KISS FOR GOOD LUCK

SATURDAY MORNING KHLOE AND I WERE UP before the sun. My phone read an eighty percent chance of snow.

"It can't snow until *after* the show," I said to Khloe and the universe. "After we're done, there can be a blizzard and I won't say a word!"

Khloe, in black-and-white polka-dot thermal pj's, ran a brush through her freshly washed and flatironed hair.

"It's not going to snow before or during the show," she declared. "I command Mother Nature!"

I laughed. "Oh, *wow*. So you can control the weather now?"

Khloe grinned. "I at least had to try, right?"

We kept up a steady stream of chatter as we got into

our show clothes. Mr. Conner wanted us dressed in our best. I'd pulled my outfit together last night. I slipped into tights, then pulled on black breeches. Two tight white tank tops went under my white show blouse. I put on my tie and secured it with a stock pin. A black blazer completed the look.

I used my boot hook to pull on my tall black boots, which I'd polished the night before. For the final touch, I slid into my black jacket, wool since it was winter, and stuck leather gloves in my pockets.

I stepped into the bathroom and checked my appearance. My blue eyes had the look they always did before a show—wide yet determined. My hair was in a neat bun at the nape of my neck, and everything looked right.

When I stepped out of the bathroom, Khloe looked over at me.

"Ready?" she asked, taking a huge breath.

"Ready."

My roommate and I zipped ourselves into hoodies that would protect our show clothes while we readied our horses. Then, together, we headed out of Hawthorne to the final show of the season.

We hurried through the cold, not saying a word. The parking lot was full of trailers, and new horses and

riders were already milling around campus. My stomach churned. It wouldn't feel better until I saw Whisper.

Inside the stable, Khloe and I skirted around horses getting last-minute touch-ups with hoof polish, students wiping their boots, and one horse half rearing as his rider tried to lead him forward.

We reached Ever's stall first.

"I'll find you before our first classes," I said.

"You better," Khloe said. She gave me a small, nervous smile.

I reached Whisper's stall and felt like I could draw my first breath since this morning.

"Hi, doll," I said. Whisper blinked sleepily.

"Hi, Laur." Lexa appeared next to me, covered in an oversize hoodie just like mine.

"Hey. You ready for this?" I asked.

Lexa's usually curly hair was in a tight bun, and her brown eyes looked a shade darker than usual. Her eyes were like mood rings. They turned different shades of brown depending on Lex's mood.

"Ready as I'll ever be," she said. Honor stuck her head over the stall door, and Lexa cupped the mare's chin in her hand.

"Honor, baby," Lexa said next to me.

We each let ourselves into our horse's stall. It was sort of an unspoken rule that once you entered your horse's stall during a show, it was private time between horse and rider. Over the stall wall, I heard Lexa murmuring to Honor. I pulled Whisper into a tight hug, giggling when she lipped softly at my earlobe.

"You're funny today," I said. "You going to be ready to go out there and show everyone how amazing you are?"

Whisper raised her head, then pushed her muzzle into my hands. I couldn't tell whether or not it had been a head bob of *yes!* or if she was fishing for a treat.

"Treat after our ride," I said. I kissed her muzzle. "Lots and lots of treats."

Whisper's winter coat was already shiny from the extra grooming I'd done last night. But there were a few stalks of hay in her mane and scattered on her withers. I checked the braids in her mane and tail; they were tight and neat even after overnight.

I clipped a lead line to her halter and led her out of the stall. Usually I kept Whisper inside while I tacked her up before a show. She didn't need the extra noise and commotion rattling her. Today, however, I wanted her to feed off the excitement of competition that pulsed through the stable.

The pair of crossties in front of her stall were free, and I clipped a tie to each side of her violet halter. I took off the lead line and hung it up outside her stall.

Inside Whisper's tack trunk, I found a body brush, hoof pick, soft blue cloth, and hoof polish. It was all I needed to get her ready.

"Let's make you sparkle!" I told her.

Starting at her poll, I worked my way all the way back to her rump, then started over on the other side. Horses and riders were everywhere—we'd been lucky to get crossties. Every pair was full now, and horses were tied to the iron stall bars and various tie rings inside and outside the stable.

I stepped back and admired Whisper's coat. "Beautiful." Every gray hair—hair that looked white—seemed to sparkle and catch the light like diamonds. I took the cloth and wiped around her eyes and muzzle. I couldn't help myself—I kissed the pink snip that I loved so much.

I pulled the hoof pick out of my pocket, stepped up to Wisp, and ran my hand down her leg.

"Hoof," I said.

Whisper lifted her leg and stood still, not resting any weight on me like some horses did.

I scraped out any hay and sawdust that had accumulated

overnight and checked to make sure her shoe was on tight. I repeated the process on the rest of her hooves. After they were clean, I grabbed clear polish and painted it onto her black-and-tan-colored hooves.

"Now, while your pretty nail polish dries," I said, "we'll get you tacked up."

Yesterday I'd spent hours cleaning her tack. There wasn't a speck of dried grass on her bit, signs of sweat on her bridle, or any dirt on her saddle pad.

I picked up the saddle and pad and settled them both onto her back. I ran the fleece-lined girth with a black stripe down the center under her belly and walked over to the other side to tighten it.

Whisper never filled her stomach with air like some horses I'd ridden had. The horses had sucked in air, tricking me into thinking the girth was tight. When I'd tried to mount, I'd slipped sideways, looking ridiculous. That had taught me to always—even with good girl Whisper—double-check the girth before my ride.

Whisper's black bridle stood out beautifully against her coat. Everything was in place.

"Now, I just have to get ready," I told Whisper. I went over to my tack trunk, unzipped my extra-long hoodie, and folded it up. I took a rag and wiped any dust off my

tall show boots. I fished out my helmet, settling the black velvet Troxel onto my head. In my right hand, I looped a crop that matched Whisper's tack around my wrist.

"You girls ready?"

I looked up to see Drew. I'd been so focused on not paying attention to the other riders that I hadn't even heard or seen him lead Polo up to us.

"Hey," I said. "You guys look great."

And they did. Drew's black hair was covered by a helmet, but he wore a crisp white shirt, black jacket, and black breeches. His show boots were as shiny as mine.

Polo, his gelding, looked as if he could beat any horse—except Wisp, of course—in the best-groomed department.

The blood bay's coat shone like deep copper. A white saddle pad matched the stocking on his hind leg and his eyes were clear and bright. He lowered his head to trade greetings with Whisper.

"Thanks," Drew said. "I was going to say the same about you two. Whisper looks as pretty as her owner."

I hid a grin, blushing. "Thank you," I said.

"Are you nervous?" Drew asked. "This is it for the year. Then we're out of competition mode until January."

"I thought I'd be nervous," I said, unhooking Wisp

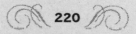

220

from the crossties. "I'm not, though. I'm calm, which is odd. I think I just feel ready, and I'm not putting pressure on myself or Whisper to get blues in both of our classes. All I care about is that we represent Canterwood well."

"I feel the same way," Drew said. His voice was smooth. "Polo's ready for anything, and there's nothing else I could have done training-wise. If we mess up today, it'll be my fault."

I held the reins under Whisper's chin. "You won't mess up. I know it."

I was standing close enough to Drew that I inhaled his minty and woodsy scent.

"I like that you believe in me," Drew whispered, inching closer. "I know you and Wisp won't disappoint anyone."

Drew and I leaned forward, still holding on to our horses, and our lips touched. His were smooth and dry, but not chapped. Zings of electricity pinged through my body. My head felt as though it was going to spin off my neck. We separated, and my grin was as wide as his.

"That's for good luck," Drew said. He winked and turned Polo around, leading him toward the stable exit.

30

ICING ON THE CONFETTI CAKE

I STOOD, ROOTED TO THE FLOOR, FOR A moment. My lips tingled like I'd applied one too many coats of Lip Venom. Finally I took a huge deep breath and walked Whisper outside. I checked her girth, mounted, and leaned down to either side to fix my stirrup leathers. I looked over as a rider in a black helmet and jacket stopped her chestnut horse beside me.

Oh, mon Dieu! Sasha Silver.

"Hey, Lauren," Sasha said, her tone friendly. The older rider looked over, smiling. Her light-brown hair was in a ponytail under her helmet. She looked so pretty in the most minimal makeup—a thin line of black eyeliner on her upper eyelids, a dusting of gray eye shadow, cheeks that needed no blush, and a coat of mascara. I was glad I'd taken my time with my own appearance this morning.

My own hair was in a neat bun, I had dusted my T-zone with powder, and I'd applied EOS lemon lip balm.

"H-hi, Sasha," I stammered. I wanted to smack my forehead. *Keep your cool!*

"I can't believe this is the last show of the season," Sasha said. She leaned down and rubbed Charm's neck. The beautiful gelding gleamed. His coat shone from hours of care and love from Sasha. He stood calm and relaxed, an ear flicked back in Sasha's direction.

Under me, I felt Whisper's muscles let go, and she dropped her head to sniff muzzles with Charm. The two horses exchanged greetings—blowing into each other's noses.

Whisper looked away, blinking. Then she glanced back shyly at Charm. Sasha and I started laughing.

"Looks like someone has a crush," I said. I patted Whisper's shoulder. "And no, I can't believe show season's over for this year either. It went by so fast."

"You're showing intermediate, right?" Sasha asked.

I nodded. "I wish Mr. Conner had offered advanced team testing before Christmas, but I can't try out for the team until I get back from break."

"You sound just like me when I was in your position," Sasha said. She focused her green eyes on me. "I was always ready to go, go, go. Always ready for the next thing. And the next thing. And whatever after that. I was terrified, of course, all along the way, but I made myself work through my fear."

"I try to model my riding after yours," I said, hoping she wouldn't think I was stalker-y.

Sasha grinned and put a hand over her heart. "I'm flattered, really. But don't try to be like me. Or at the very least, don't try to be like *that* version of me."

"Why? Look where you ended up."

"It's not that I'm not grateful to be where I am or unhappy about any of the choices I made," Sasha answered. "But there are some things I wish I'd done a little different. Like slow down. Enjoy the moment and savor where I am. Be happy about my current accomplishment and not push myself to be ready for the next hurdle."

I nodded, taking in her every word.

"I was so eager to get to the advanced team and then the Youth Equestrian National Team that I was superstressed all of the time. I wanted everything to move faster, and I always felt like I had to catch up."

"To who?" I asked.

Sasha shifted Charm's reins into one hand and relaxed her posture. "To no one, actually. I thought that because I was from Union and had no training, I had to be at a certain level to even be noticed against my friends—riders like Callie Harper and Heather Fox."

"I've heard of them," I said. "I heard rumors that Heather's your arch-nemesis or something."

Sasha waved a hand in the air. "Ancient history. That's part of what I'm talking about—stressing over the wrong things, like my 'war' against Heather. We wasted so much time pitting ourselves against each other. If we'd just applied that to riding, we would been so much better for it."

I considered everything Sasha said. She was wise beyond her years, and I'd be an idiot not to take every morsel of advice from her that I could. Around us, horses and riders headed toward different arenas to wait for the start of their classes. I was glad to have Sasha distracting me from worrying about the show.

"Honestly, I can't imagine ever getting to where you are in your head. I'm constantly trying to do just what you said—be ready for the next thing and train around the clock." Whisper shifted her back legs. "I feel like I'll always be the new girl from Union, with a background that I have to live up to."

"Your background doesn't define who you are now," Sasha said. She smiled at me. "*You*, in this moment, define yourself. You're not the new girl. You're not the Union girl. Or the dressage champion girl. You're the Canterwood girl. You're Lauren Towers, intermediate rider."

I grinned. "I like how that sounds."

Sasha laughed. "I know exactly what you mean. Don't let old memories from the past alter how you approach your classes today. It doesn't mean you can forget everything, but you have to try and leave it where it belongs—in the past."

I took a deep breath. "In the past."

"Embrace who you are, Lauren," Sasha said. "The Lauren you are now is pretty darn cool."

I blushed. I couldn't believe Sasha had just said that!

"Thank you so much," I said.

"My dreams came true the day I got my acceptance letter to Canterwood," Sasha said. "Everything else—every passed class, every ribbon, every good lesson—it's all icing on a giant confetti cake."

Her words made me smile. "You're right. I am so lucky to be here and, in contrast to what you just said, every failed test, lost ribbon, bad lesson—those are all things that can be improved. What better place to do it than Canterwood?"

"I know that you and I both tried *so* hard to get here," Sasha said. She looked over at me. "Sometimes I think we forget and don't appreciate that we have something people dream of."

"I never want to take Canterwood for granted," I said. "If I ever do, I don't deserve to be here."

"Agreed. Every sacrifice we made to get here was worth it. It paid off and we, two girls from Union, Connecticut, are enrolled at one of the most prestigious boarding schools on the East Coast and training with one extremely talented instructor."

"I don't regret a second of the clichéd blood, sweat, and tears that it took me to get here." I smiled, shaking my head slightly. "And there were a *lot* of tears."

"There's no telling if your future will be full of more tears *or* laughs," Sasha said. "My future is just as uncertain. I could fall off Charm and break my arm tomorrow. But our lives would be just as unpredictable no matter where we were."

"Absolutely. If we both still rode at Briar Creek, we wouldn't have a crystal ball to tell us where we'd be today or tomorrow." I leaned forward and stroked Whisper's neck.

"I wouldn't want my future to be determined anywhere but here," Sasha declared.

"Me either," I said.

We sat in silence for a moment. I looked out across the arenas, parking lot, stable, and pens. Dozens of horses walked, trotted, and cantered on the grounds. Riders put their horses through half-passes, jumped over tall oxers, and walked along the fence of the big arena. Shiny trailers filled the parking lot, and riders and their instructors loaded and unloaded bundled-up horses from the trailers. Mr. Conner, crutches and all, motioned for a group of younger riders to enter one of the warm-up rings.

Finally I looked at the stable. The black-and-white barn I'd stared at, wide-eyed, on my first day here. The white with black trim looked as if it had just been washed. A few horses were tied to the outdoor tie rings and being tacked up. Horses that weren't being showed today had their heads over stall windows, taking in the busyness outside. The stable didn't look overwhelming and frightening like it did on day one. Now it looked like Whisper's home. Just like Canterwood was mine.

After break, I was coming back with a new attitude. I wanted to take Sasha's advice to heart. I'd follow my dreams, but I wouldn't rush through one phase of my life here just to get to the next. I'd worked hard to get

to Canterwood, and I owed it to myself to take in every second of my accomplishment. I was prepared to work through the bad spots, too. Even if I failed a test, it didn't mean I should drop that class. Even if I had a bad riding lesson, it didn't mean I deserved to berate myself for days. I couldn't wait for January, when I could have a fresh start with a new semester.

The loudspeaker crackled. "And now," a voice said, "may we please have intermediate riders competing in the dressage class to arena A and members of our YENT to arena D."

Sasha and I looked at each other.

"That's us," Sasha said. She picked up the reins, and her movements woke up Charm. He looked ready to go.

Sasha reached into her jacket pocket, pulled out a watermelon Lip Smacker, and smoothed it over her lips.

I laughed. "Now that's a rumor confirmed! You are a gloss addict!"

Giggling and giving a *who me?* shrug, Sasha offered it to me. I took it from her, putting on the smooth gloss.

I handed it back to her, and Sasha squeezed my hand. "It's my lucky gloss," she said. "I'd wish you luck, but you don't need it. You have talent on your side."

I smiled my thanks to the girl who, whether she wanted to believe it or not, had changed my life in more ways than she'd ever know.

"Team Canterwood!" Sasha cheered.

"For the win!" I chimed in.

ABOUT THE AUTHOR

Twenty-five-year-old Jessica Burkhart (a.k.a. Jess Ashley) writes from Brooklyn, New York. She's obsessed with sparkly things, lip gloss, and TV. She loves hanging with her bestie, watching too much TV, and shopping for all things Hello Kitty. Learn more about Jess at www.JessicaBurkhart.com. Find everything Canterwood Crest at www.CanterwoodCrest.com.